LAMBERT'S LADY

SLEEPER SEALS, BOOK 13

SUSAN STOKER

D1247553

Edited by Kelli Collins

Cover Design by Chris Mackey, AURA Design Group

Manufactured in the United States

A Note to the Reader

A special thank you to every reader who picked up any of the Sleeper SEAL books! It was very fun collaborating with all the authors to get this series written.

The common thread for each of the books in the Sleeper SEAL series is, of course, Commander Greg Lambert. We knew when we started that he would also need his Happily Ever After.

I am thrilled to be able to give it to you!

It's short, sweet, and oh so kick butt.

This story can be read at any point in the series. It's written from the standpoint of Greg Lambert AFTER all 12 former SEALs have been successful in their missions he's given them, but if you can't wait until you've read all 12 books, you can read it early!

CHAPTER ONE

Lambert's Lady

*R*etired Navy Commander Greg Lambert hung up the phone and leaned back in his chair. Putting his arms behind his head, he stared sightlessly at the phone he'd just put down on his desktop. He'd heard thirty minutes ago from the twelfth sleeper SEAL he'd hired to combat home-grown terrorism. He'd been successful in taking down another terrorist who'd planned an attack on fellow Americans.

Not only that, but the former Navy SEAL informed Greg that he'd found the love of his life. Greg smiled. They all had. Every single one of the twelve men he'd hired to take down terrorists who'd infiltrated their country had somehow managed to find a woman who completed him, and who had no issues standing by his side.

He hadn't started out to be a matchmaker, but it felt damn good to know men he respected and admired had been able to let down their guards enough to find happiness.

And that led him to thinking about his own life. His kids were grown and living lives of their own. His wife, Karen, had died almost five years ago from cancer. He'd expected to retire from the Navy and spend the rest of his life with her. Traveling the world and relaxing and for once, not worrying about politics or what the terrorists were doing now.

That wasn't the way it turned out, and Greg had been bitter for a long time. But his friends—the Vice President of the United States, the Secretary of State, and the highest-ranking man in the CIA—had come to him and begged him to organize and hire the Sleeper SEALs to combat terrorism.

Sitting up suddenly, Greg moved toward the door. Ever since his first Sleeper SEAL had called to inform him that the assigned threat had been neutralized, he'd gone out for a celebratory drink after each mission. Now that the twelfth and final

SEAL had reported in, he was eager to have that drink.

Greg shook his head at himself. No, he wasn't eager for the drink. He was eager to see the woman who *made* that drink.

Sheridan Temple.

At first, he hadn't paid much attention to the gregarious and outgoing bartender. He'd been content to sit at the bar and soak up the ambiance of the place. But little by little, as he'd visited the hole-in-the-wall bar for his celebratory drinks, he'd begun talking to her...and realized that his libido hadn't died with his beloved wife after all.

Sheridan was younger than him by quite a bit. She had long dark blonde hair that she freely admitted to keeping that way by making bi-monthly visits to her hairdresser. She was rounded in all the right places, namely her tits and ass. She smiled all the time and made Greg relax simply by being near him.

When he first went to the bar, he'd ordered his bourbon, drank it, and left. Slowly over the months, however, he'd nursed his drink and talked with Sheridan. Now every time he visited, he closed down the bar and walked the pretty bartender home, making sure no one messed with her as she traveled the two blocks to her apartment.

Greg had planned on being alone for the rest of this life. Even his departed wife's mean ol' Chihuahua had finally passed away at the age of fifteen and a half a couple months ago. But with every visit to Sheridan's bar, he realized that he wanted more.

And he knew Sheridan did too.

She'd come right out and told him so one night.

He'd walked her home, and as they were standing in front of her apartment doors, she'd surprised him by standing up on tiptoe and kissing him.

She might've made the first move, but Greg wasn't an idiot. He'd immediately kissed her back, pressing her against the wall of her apartment building.

After several minutes of making out like teenagers, she'd pulled back and looked him straight in the eye. "I want more."

"More what?" Greg had asked.

"More than long talks at the bar and you walking me home. I want you to come up and spend the night. I want to cook you breakfast, wearing only your shirt, and have the right to call you whenever I feel like it."

Greg had blinked and stared at her like an idiot. "You do?"

She'd smiled at him. "Yeah, Greg. I do. Think about it. I'll see you later."

That conversation had happened a month ago, and Greg had done a lot of thinking since then. He'd been hesitant because of his job as leader of the Ghost Ops. The Sleeper SEALs. But now that it was done, he felt comfortable enough to go after what he wanted for the second time in his life. Screw politics. Screw doing what everyone thought he should. He wanted to spend the night in Sheridan's bed and have her spend the night in his. He wanted her in his kitchen, making him that breakfast, and wanted the right to come up behind her and bend her over the table and show her how much he appreciated it.

He might not be twenty-five anymore, but he'd masturbated to the thought of having Sheridan's lush curves under him, and over him, and in his shower, and bent over his couch, every night since she'd told him she wanted to be with him.

Tonight was the night. He was free of his obligation to the CIA—and he was going to tell Sheridan that she was his.

A smile spread over Greg's face as he left his condo. He couldn't wait.

* * *

Sheridan Temple was tired and a little heartsick. Figured that the first man she'd gotten up the nerve to tell exactly what she wanted had run and not looked back after she'd done it.

Greg Lambert was the sexiest man she'd ever seen, and that was saying a lot, since she worked as a bartender and had seen plenty of good looking men. But there was just something about Greg that did it for her. His black hair was too long—he'd admitted to liking it that way, since he'd always had to keep it shorn close to his head when he was in the Navy. He had a beard and mustache, and Sheridan wondered more than once how it would feel brushing against her inner thighs. He looked younger than his fifty years, even with the bit of gray showing in his beard. He was slender yet muscular, and a few inches taller than she was.

But more than his good looks, it was his take-charge attitude that made her wet between her legs.

At first, he'd just been another customer. But as she'd gotten to know him, he'd become more to her.

She knew he was retired from the Navy and still working as a consultant in some form or another with the government. She knew he was a widow and had a couple of grown kids. She knew he liked to drink expensive bourbon, and that he was a breast man. She hadn't missed the way his eyes were drawn to her cleavage every time she bent over to get a glass or pick up something that had fallen on the floor.

But what really got to her was that he saw *her*. He didn't look down on her because she was a bartender in a piece-of-crap bar. He didn't seem to care that she was older than the other bartenders at the bar. When she'd brought it up, he'd simply asked, "Do you enjoy it?" And when she said that she did, he'd replied, "Then screw what everyone thinks."

She'd pretty much fallen head over heels for him right then.

But it had taken another couple of months for her to get up the courage to make a move. It was obvious he was too much of a gentleman to do it himself. So one night, after he'd walked her home, she'd taken a deep breath and kissed him.

And what a kiss.

Sheridan had been married once. Granted, it had only lasted for four years before she'd divorced the cheating asshole, but she'd had her share of men. But one kiss from Greg Lambert and she was gone.

She might've instigated the kiss, but he'd immediately taken over. She still remembered the feel of his hand at the nape of her neck, holding her still as he devoured her mouth. His beard and mustache were surprisingly soft against her face. As he kissed her, his free hand had moved up to rest on her side, his thumb brushing the underside of her boob. He hadn't gotten fresh with her, but oh how she'd wanted him to.

Her only excuse for what she'd said after he'd finally pulled back was that her brain was still short-circuited from that kiss. She'd told him that she wanted him. That she wanted to cook him breakfast, practically naked. She was such an idiot.

Obviously she was an idiot, because she hadn't seen him since, when he'd been coming in at least twice a week for the last few months.

Sighing, wanting to be anywhere but at the bar, Sheridan pasted on the fake smile she'd perfected over the last month and turned toward the door when the little bell rang, announcing another arrival.

"Evenin'," she called out. "Sit anywhere you want. Someone will be with you in a moment."

The last word was barely out of her mouth when she realized it was none other than the object of her late-night fantasies, Greg Lambert, who had walked in the door.

Flustered, Sheridan wasn't sure what to do. She wanted to be coy and cool, but since she hadn't seen him since her embarrassing proposal, she couldn't do anything but stand stock still.

Greg walked straight for her, his dark eyes piercing in their intensity. She couldn't look away.

He came right up to the bar and leaned toward her. "Come here."

Sheridan's brows furrowed. She took a step closer to him, the large bar top still between them. She held a glass in one hand and a warm dishrag in the other. She'd been washing and rinsing the glasses for use later.

When she got close enough, Greg reached out and took her face between his hands and pulled her toward him. Sheridan stumbled, but her belly hit the edge of the bar, steading her.

Without a word, Greg leaned down and kissed her.

Not a peck on the lips either. His tongue ran along the seam of her lips until she opened for him, and then he plunged inside. Sheridan's eyes closed and she leaned closer, letting him hold her steady as he publically laid claim to her.

Her eyes opened as his lips left hers, and she was aware the other patrons in the bar were cheering and clapping. She knew her cheeks were probably red, but she refused to break eye contact with Greg.

"Yes," he said huskily, licking his bottom lip sensuously. "I want that too."

"What?" Sheridan asked in confusion.

"You. In my bed. In my kitchen. Under me, over me, any way I can get you."

"Oh."

He grinned and ran his thumb along her jawline, making her shiver all over again. "Is the offer still open?"

Sheridan cleared her throat. "Depends."

"On?"

"On whether or not it took a month for you to talk yourself into it, or a month for you to try to talk yourself out of it."

He chuckled and let go. She immediately felt the loss of his touch but forced herself to stand up straight. She wasn't sure he understood what she meant by her words. She didn't want him if he had to force himself to date her. She knew he had baggage, she did too. But him not coming to the bar for a month wasn't exactly the reaction she'd had in mind when she'd propositioned him.

"I didn't stay away because you had the balls to make the first move, Sher," Greg said, and she almost melted at the term of endearment. "I didn't need to talk myself into *or* out of wanting you. That's always been a given. I've wanted you since that first time we closed down the bar together."

"Why *did* you stay away then?"

"I'm free," he said.

Sheridan frowned in confusion. "Free?"

"My last commitment has been cleared up. I got the call tonight."

She nodded. He'd told her the very basics, enough for her to know he was in charge of a group of men who were doing top-secret things to keep the country safe. "Good."

"Since I'm free, I can concentrate on other things. On you, Sher. I can concentrate on you."

Another shiver ran through her. His gaze dropped for just a moment, from her eyes to her chest, then back up. She smiled. "Is that so?"

"Yeah. So the answer is yes."

"I'm not a one-night stand," she warned, putting the now dry glass down.

It was his turn to frown. His eyes turned angry.

"Damn straight you aren't," he said immediately. "We're both too old for that shit."

"So we're what? Friends with benefits?" she asked, wanting to get it all straight now so she could guard her heart from falling in love with him if he wasn't looking for the same.

Greg leaned forward again, and Sheridan held her breath, eager to hear his answer.

But just then, a man four barstools down from them called out, "I need another one, Sheridan. That is, if you're done eye-fucking the commander there."

Others around them laughed, and Sheridan couldn't help but roll her eyes. The men and women who came to the bar night after night were practically family, but right then she could've killed ol' Jack. She turned her head and yelled, "Keep your shirt on. Jeez."

"Go on," Greg said, stepping to the left and taking a seat on what she considered "his" barstool. "This can wait."

She wanted to disagree. Wanted to tell him that, no, it couldn't wait. That she wanted to know what he was going to classify their relationship as...but instead she simply nodded. "You want your usual?"

Greg nodded. "Celebrating tonight, Sher. And not just the success of my latest victory."

She understood what he meant and smiled shyly.

"Be back with your bourbon, Greg."

"I'll be here."

Sheridan nodded and turned away from him to get Jack another beer. But she made sure to shake her ass a little more as she did it...just in case Greg was watching.

* * *

G reg sipped his bourbon and was hard-pressed to take his eyes off of Sheridan. Tonight she was wearing a tight pair of jeans that hugged her legs as if they were painted on. Her ass looked delicious, and he couldn't wait to feel her thighs wrapped around his hips as he took her. His late wife had been slender. Almost too slender. She'd constantly been worried about her looks and what the other officer's wives and the snakes of Washington thought about her. Greg had reassured her that loved her exactly the way she was. Karen was funny, smart, and never failed to have a good comeback when someone tried to be snarky with her.

On the surface, Sheridan looked nothing like his deceased wife. She had curves that went on for miles and she didn't give two shits what others thought about her. He'd seen her knock catty women down with simply a look when they dared say disparaging things about her to their friends. Sheridan was nearing forty, over a decade younger than him, but Greg could honestly say he'd never been as hard for a woman as he was right then.

The black tank top she had on was tight and hugged her tits. Every time she bent over, he could see her cleavage. And he swore she was bending over more and more, simply to torment him.

He hadn't missed the worried look on her face when she'd asked if he wanted to be friends with benefits. He'd been two seconds away from reassuring her when Jack had interrupted. He'd been pissed at first, but now he was enjoying teasing her. Sheridan was no one's fuck buddy. She was made to be cherished. It was obvious she worked hard; she was at the bar almost every night. She'd told him that she had plenty of money saved up from her previous job, but was bored and had taken the bartending job to have something to do.

In other words, she was lonely.

Just like him.

And Greg wanted to make sure she was never lonely again. By keeping her. Forever.

No, he didn't want to be friends with benefits. He wanted her to move in with him, or he could move in with her if she preferred. He didn't give a shit. He'd purchased his condo after Karen had died because he didn't like the memories in their home of the hell she'd gone through, fighting the cancer.

He would always miss Karen, but Sheridan was so different from his deceased wife. She was outgoing where Karen had been shy. Sheridan wasn't afraid to go toe-to-toe with an unruly patron, while Karen would've stepped back to avoid confrontation.

Greg had been conflicted about his feelings for Sheridan for a long time. In the last month, he'd purposely stayed away from her and done some deep thinking. In that time, he recalled one of the last things Karen had told him. She'd begged him to keep on living. To not mourn her for the rest of his life. She had wanted him to be happy. To experience all the things they didn't get to. She'd hated the thought of him being alone.

Greg had loved Karen. Had thought they'd grow

old together and his attraction to Sheridan had come as a surprise, even with Karen's requests for him to fall in love again and move on with his life.

But what had truly made up his mind was how much he missed Sheridan over the last month since he'd seen her. He missed bantering with her. Seeing her smile and laugh. He just plain missed being around her.

Greg sat on the barstool and watched Sheridan for the rest of the night. She joked with him and they'd talked when she had some down time, but there was a new current of sexual awareness between them tonight that hadn't been there before. Greg had been semi-hard all night and couldn't wait to walk her home.

Finally, she was done cleaning and straightening the bar, the manager had removed the money from the cash register, and she'd pocketed her tips for the night.

"Ready?" Greg asked quietly.

She nodded.

Greg held out his hand and, without hesitation, even though they'd never done this before, she took it in her own. Greg intertwined their fingers and squeezed, telling her without words how happy he was that she was by his side. She smiled at him and they walked out into the dark night, turning to the right toward her apartment without words.

"So?" she asked after a couple of minutes. "You gonna answer my question or what?"

Greg smirked. "What question?"

She stopped and tried to tug her hand out of his, but he refused to let go.

"You know what question. You said this isn't a one-night stand, but what do you want? Just to fuck when you have the time? When you decide to grace me with your presence?"

Getting serious, Greg pulled Sheridan closer. He wrapped his free hand around the back of her head and bunched her hair in his palm before gripping it tightly. He wasn't hurting her, but he also wanted to make sure he had her complete attention before he said what he had to say. "How many men have you met at the bar and taken home?"

Her eyes widened before they narrowed. Then she started to struggle in his grip. Trying to get away from him. "Let me go, asshole."

"Answer me, Sher. How many?"

"You know how many."

"Humor me."

She glared at him. "None."

"Right. None. Except for me. And if you think

whatever it is we have is casual, you're insane. I've spent the last month jacking off thinking about finally getting to see your tits. About having you half naked in my kitchen, like you said you wanted. This is not casual. We are not fuck buddies. We are dating. And Sher, my intention is to date you for as long as you're comfortable with before putting my ring on your finger and making you mine in a way that no one can mistake."

Greg wanted to smile at the look in her eyes, the complete and utter shock, but he didn't. He was too worried about what she was going to say and do next.

* * *

*S*heridan stared at Greg in disbelief. She didn't think he'd be a dick about hooking up with her, but the last thing she'd expected was for him to practically ask her to marry him. "Seriously?"

"Yeah, Sher. Seriously. I wouldn't have said it if I didn't mean it."

"Oh."

"Got any more questions for me before we go

back to your place and you have your wicked way with me?"

Sheridan liked the thought of that, but she wanted to get one more thing straight. "Are you gonna give me your phone number?"

He blinked. "What?"

"Your number. I want it. After all this time of us getting to know each other at the bar, you never offered me your number, nor asked for mine. I don't want to have to wait a month for you to show back up at the bar before getting to talk to you again."

Greg growled. The sound that came out of his throat couldn't be described as anything else. He tightened his hand in her hair—Sheridan had to admit that it was exciting as hell, him holding her like that—and leaned in. "Woman. What did I just say?"

She opened her mouth to answer, but he didn't give her a chance.

"I said that we weren't fuck buddies and that I wanted to marry you. I'm not going to go one day without seeing you, much less a month. I had to wait for my commitments to be fulfilled before I could come for you. But now that I'm here, I'm *here*. Got it?"

"So does that mean you're gonna give me your number?" Sheridan asked cheekily.

"Yeah, Sher. You're gonna get my number… among other things I'm gonna give you," he returned.

Sheridan giggled. "Okay."

"Shit, you're a pain," he said, but since he was smiling as he said it, Sheridan didn't take offense. He moved his hand from the back of her head, caressing her nape briefly, and turned toward her apartment.

They'd taken only a few steps when Greg suddenly stopped.

Sheridan stumbled against him, not understanding what was happening. Her attention had been on Greg and not on their surroundings.

"Give me your wallet," a gruff voice demanded.

Sheridan gasped and looked up. A teenager had stepped out of an alley and now stood in front of them, holding a knife, gesturing at Greg impatiently.

She felt Greg loosen his hold on her hand and she dropped it, feeling nervous but not quite alarmed. Yet.

"I said, give me your wallet, old man," the boy repeated.

Greg held up his hands in a consolatory gesture.

"You don't want to do this," he told the teenager. "Just turn around and leave."

The boy laughed. A low, mean sound that grated on Sheridan's nerves. "As if. Give me your wallet *now*." He turned to Sheridan. "And you, bitch, I want all your jewelry."

"I'm not wearing any," Sheridan told him honestly. She never wore jewelry when she worked at the bar. She knew she'd be walking home and never wanted to provoke anyone into robbing her. Fat lot of good *that* did her.

The teenager looked confused for a second before saying, "Your money then. I want all of it."

Thinking about the tips she'd earned that night, Sheridan grimaced, but started to reach into her back pocket to pull out the wallet she kept there. She generally didn't carry a purse either, for the same reason she didn't wear jewelry. She loved bags, had a ton of them at home, but never carried one when she knew she'd be walking on the city streets late at night.

Greg grabbed her wrist and prevented her from pulling out her wallet. "Seriously, kid. You picked the wrong couple to rob. Turn around and leave and I'll forget this happened."

"What are you gonna do?" the kid taunted.

"You're older than dirt. You ain't shit. Now, give me your fucking money or I'll cut her." He thrust the knife in Sheridan's direction menacingly.

She took a step away from him, not liking the crazed look in his eye. "Maybe we should—"

It was all she got out before Greg struck.

If she hadn't been standing right there watching, she wouldn't have believed it, but within seconds, Greg had disarmed the punk kid and had him on the ground. One arm was wrenched behind his back and Greg's knee was pressed to his spine, holding him down. The kid was cursing and kicking but couldn't break the hold Greg had on him.

"Sher, can you please grab my phone from my back pocket and call the police for me?"

She blinked. He'd sounded so calm and matter-of-fact.

"Sheridan?"

The sound of Greg calling her name got her moving. She jumped forward and pulled his cell phone out of his pocket.

"The code is one, two, three, four, five, six."

"Oh my God. It is not."

He turned his head to look at her and grinned. "Yup. I forget anything else."

Sheridan rolled her eyes. She knew the man

didn't forget anything, but she was still a little surprised that it unlocked after she pushed in the numbers. "That's the worst password in the history of passwords," she mumbled as she dialed 9-1-1.

After she'd informed the dispatcher of the situation, and that Greg had things under control, she looked back down at the man she couldn't wait to get into her bed and asked, "Should we be worried about anyone else surprising us?"

Greg shrugged. "Not sure. But I'll handle it if they do."

Sheridan should've been annoyed by his cockiness, but instead she simply nodded. She had no doubt Greg would be able to "handle it" if the punk's friends showed up. He'd taken down the teenager as if he did this every day, and he wasn't even breathing hard.

Every time she learned something new about the man, she wanted him more. She'd never felt safer than when she was by Greg's side. Tonight just underscored that tenfold.

"Let me up!" the teenager cried out.

Greg chuckled but it wasn't humorous. "Riiiiight. After you threatened to cut my woman, you think I'm gonna let you up? I don't think so."

"Not to mention he called you old," Sheridan reminded him helpfully.

"Man, I didn't mean it."

Sheridan laughed. After looking around and seeing no one else sneaking up on them, she crouched down next to the kid. He was grimacing from the way Greg was holding his arm behind his back and pressing him into the concrete. He squirmed, which was totally ineffective at getting Greg to loosen his hold. "You picked the wrong man to mess with," Sheridan told the teenager.

"Whatever," the boy whined.

"He told you to walk away," she reminded the kid gleefully, not above rubbing it in that he was taken down so easily.

"Stay still," Greg warned, then indicated with his head for Sheridan to back away from him.

She stood and took a step back. She wasn't afraid of the kid now. There was no way Greg was going to let him go.

"He's a Navy SEAL," Sheridan informed the teen. "A decorated war veteran, a retired commander, and he personally knows both the President and Vice President of the United States. Not to mention, he's also worked for the CIA and who knows what other top-secret badass organizations. I have no doubt he could break your arm with a twist of his hand and have you blubbering like a little baby. And just to be clear, that *old man* just kicked your teenage ass. Show some respect," she spat. "You want money? Earn it your damn self. Get off the streets and get a job, for goodness sake," she told him. "Robbing people of their hard-earned money doesn't make you tough—it makes you a bully and an asshole."

"Fuck you," the teenager replied, then screamed in pain when Greg did something to his arm.

"I don't think he's gonna listen to you," Greg informed her mildly.

Sheridan rolled her eyes and shook her head. "What a waste. Seriously. I don't get why people think it's okay to hurt others. Rob them, break into houses, rape people. It's just crazy. Why can't everyone just be nice? Is that so freaking hard?"

If anything, Greg smiled bigger. "I can be nice."

Sheridan blew out a breath and tried to relax. "Yeah?"

"Reaaaaal nice."

She smiled.

Sirens were heard in the distance and they both turned their heads to look that way.

Thirty minutes later, after Greg had gotten up off the teenager and let the cop take him away, and after giving their statements, and after refusing any kind of medical treatment since neither of them had been hurt, they were finally on their way to Sheridan's apartment.

They didn't speak, but when they got to the door, Greg stopped her. "Are you okay? We can wait if you're upset about what happened."

Sheridan turned to him and stared. She wasn't sure why he was asking. She didn't think she'd been putting out vibes that said she was upset. Maybe he'd changed his mind? Biting her lip, she asked uncertainly, "Do *you* want to wait?"

In response, Greg pushed her up against the wall and cradled her head in his large palms.

Sheridan was beginning to think that was his go-to way of making sure she was paying attention, but what he didn't realize was that she was *always* paying attention to him. She couldn't do anything *but* pay attention to him when he was around.

"I'm so on edge, I could take you right here, right now," he said in a low, rumbly tone. "The thought of that punk-ass kid threatening you with that knife makes me so pissed off, I can barely stand it."

"You didn't seem mad," Sheridan told him, reaching up and gripping his wrists.

"That's because I was in control. The one thing

SEALs are taught is to stay in control. But I don't *feel* in control right now. I need you, Sheridan."

His words made her belly feel tight. It had been a very long time since anyone had needed her. Wanted her? Yes. *Needed* her? No.

Without a word, she squeezed his wrists and pulled his hands from her face. Then she interlaced her fingers with his and pulled him toward the door.

He followed without a word as she towed him into her building and down the hall toward the stairs. She walked up two flights and down the hall to her door. When she pulled out her key, he took it from her, unlocking the knob and the bolt then holding her door open. The second the door closed, Sheridan turned and pulled Greg to her.

* * *

*G*reg was holding on by a thread. He'd had no doubt that he could easily take the thug on the street, but still, the chance of the kid getting lucky and hurting Sheridan before Greg could disarm him was still fresh in his mind. The way she hadn't panicked, had trusted him to take care of the situation, and even how she'd told off the kid, praising him at the same time, had made him want her all the more.

He'd tried to do the right thing, give her a chance to think about what was going to happen between them. The last thing he wanted was for her to be with him tonight because of adrenaline or some other misguided reason, but instead she'd pulled him into her building.

He'd planned on getting her something to drink and sitting on her couch and talking for a while, but instead she'd grabbed him and kissed him.

The second her lips touched his, he knew he was a goner. He'd wanted to go slow, but that was thrown right out the window. He wanted her. Bad. And somehow, he'd gotten lucky enough for her to want him right back.

Sheridan moaned under her breath and their teeth knocked together as they fought to get inside each other's mouths.

"Clothes...off," she ordered between kisses.

Greg wasn't one to take orders, but that was one he'd gladly obey. He took a step back, and his hands went to the buttons on his shirt. She followed him, their mouths still glued together.

Pulling back, he said, "Arms up."

She immediately raised her arms above her head and he pulled the tank top up her body and over her head. Her hair fell around her shoulders in disarray as her hands immediately went to his own shirt and he let her push it off his shoulders.

Greg stared at her tits as her hands went to his jeans. He couldn't move. Couldn't breathe. His dick was pressed so hard against his zipper it hurt, but he still couldn't do anything other than stare at her tits. She was wearing a black lace bra and her mounds of flesh were almost overflowing the cups. Her cleavage was impressive, and his hands moved without thought.

He cupped her then, squeezing hard enough for her hands to still at his waistband as she threw her head back and moaned in delight.

"God, Greg...yes."

With no thought in his mind other than finally seeing her, Greg roughly pulled the cups down and dropped his head. He sucked on her exposed nipple. Ate at it as if he were a starving man. She arched and one of her hands went to the back of his head. He felt her fingernails dig into his scalp as she pressed him closer.

"Yesssss," she hissed.

As he devoured her breast, he pinched her other

nipple with his free hand, rolling it until it was a hard little point. Then he switched sides, biting, sucking, and nibbling at her flesh until one leg came up and she pressed her hips into him desperately.

When she began to hump against him, Greg finally pulled back and looked down. Her upper chest was flushed with desire and her breasts were plumped up by her bra, her nipples hard and begging him to play further.

"You are so fucking beautiful," Greg said reverently.

"Please, Greg. More."

"Oh, you'll get more, Sher," he told her. Then swooped down and started kissing her again. He walked them both backwards as he undid the button on her jeans. When she almost tripped over the material he'd shoved down her thighs, he stopped and let her shove them the rest of the way off, along with her socks and shoes.

He fumbled at his own jeans as they entered the living area. Not wanting to lose contact with her for a second, he swore under his breath when he had to reach down and get rid of his shoes to get his jeans off.

Sheridan reached behind her to remove her bra and he barked, "Leave it."

Greg knew he was being too bossy. But he couldn't help it. He loved how her tits were pushed up by the bra and wanted to take her just like that.

He shoved his boxers down his hips and ignored her gasp as his cock sprang up between them. He could feel precome leaking from the tip and knew it smeared on her belly as he took a step into her. He pushed her panties down as far as he could reach, and she took care of getting them the rest of the way off.

Greg put one hand on the small of her back and the other on her ass and supported her as he pushed her down to the couch and followed, keeping his weight off her. She went without complaint, a small smile on her face.

"This is gonna be fast, Sher," he said with a straight face. "I need you too badly to go slow."

"Fast is fine," she gasped, as his hand moved between her legs.

"You're soaked, sweetheart," he said in awe as his fingers swept between her folds, spreading the excitement he found there up to her clit.

"How could I not be?" she asked, clinging to his biceps tightly. "You taking that guy down as if he were no more than a pesky bug was a total turn-on."

Greg smiled. "You weren't scared?"

"With you by my side, absolutely not?"

Her words made Greg feel ten feet tall. Yeah, he'd been a SEAL, but that was years ago. He'd done so much political crap since then, he'd felt as if he'd lost the respect he used to have as a member of the Special Forces team.

He slowly pressed one finger inside her tight sheath, gritting his teeth at how soft and wet she was inside.

Sheridan lifted her hips toward him as much as she could and moaned. "More."

Instead of giving her more, he moved his soaked finger up to her clit and began rubbing her there. "You'll get more of me," he told her. "But you come first. Always."

"Oh shit," she said, even as she started moving her hips under his finger. Greg brought his free hand down to his dick and squeezed the base, hard. He was about ready to blow, but he wanted to be inside her when he did.

"You're so beautiful," he said as he eyed the bounty of female flesh under him. He loved her curves. Loved the way her tits shook and shifted with the movement of her hips. Her belly had a little pooch and he couldn't wait to explore and caress every inch of her body. Later. "God, yes, that's it," he murmured as she writhed on his hand. "Show me what you like."

"Harder," she ordered. "Finger me harder."

Greg did, loving the smell of her arousal that wafted up between them. Her tits were jiggling and moving against his chest, her nipples catching on his chest hair as she ground against him.

He felt her legs tense and her belly quake even as she said, "I'm gonna come!" Greg pressed harder and faster against her stiff bundle of nerves and watched in awe as her back arched, and then her legs squeezed his hips as she came.

Her orgasm was a thing of beauty, and Greg wanted to see it again and again and again. He let go and began to fumble beside them for his jeans. It was tough because his other hand was still firmly grasping his dick. His orgasm was a heartbeat away and he was hanging on by a thread.

"What are you doing?" she asked, running her hands up and down his chest, doing nothing to help his control.

"Condom," he bit out between clenched teeth.

"I'm on the pill," she told him. "Have been for years."

Greg stilled and turned back to her. "What are you saying?" he asked.

"Were you serious about wanting me for more than a fast fuck?"

Greg clenched his teeth and braced his body above hers, his dick forgotten for the moment. "Of course I was. I wouldn't say it if I didn't mean it."

"I want to be yours," Sheridan told him. "The last month was unbearable, not having you around. I missed you something awful. I like talking to you. I like watching you smile and laugh with the others in the bar. I feel more like a woman around you than I have in my entire life. I don't know what will happen between us...but I want to give a relationship a try. I trust you. Fuck me, Greg."

He stared at her in disbelief. "I'm clean, Sher. Swear on it. You really trust me?"

She nodded. "I've only been with one man bare, and he was my husband. Of course, he screwed me over, big time, and I haven't trusted anyone since. But I trust *you*, Greg Lambert. With my safety, which you proved you deserved tonight. And now with my body. I'm yours for as long as you want me."

Greg was moving before she finished speaking. The head of his cock needing no assistance in getting to where it wanted to go. He was halfway inside her before he managed to control his thrust.

"Shit. Fuck. Damn it," he murmured under his breath. "Am I hurting you?"

"It's been a while...you're big," Sheridan said on a gasp. "But you're not hurting me."

Greg pulled back and then eased forward slower, pushing in a bit farther. Then he did it again, and again, until finally he could feel her small strip of pubic hair against his belly.

His cock throbbed, as if it had a heartbeat of its own. "You're so fucking hot," Greg told Sheridan as he held himself still inside her.

"Move," she begged, trying to shift under him, but not getting far because of his body weight on hers.

"I can't," he admitted.

She looked up at him and he saw the alarm in her gaze. "Why not?"

"Because if I move, I'm gonna come."

She grinned and ran her fingernails down his back until she reached his ass. Then she squeezed his butt cheeks and pressed him harder into her. "It's okay."

"It's not okay," he countered, gritting his teeth. "I want this to last."

"Next time," she murmured, leaning up and taking his earlobe between her ears.

"Oh fuck," he swore, then dropped to his elbows over her. Her tongue licking his ear was the last straw. He couldn't hold back.

"I'll make it up to you," he told her, even as he brought his hips back and thrust hard inside her once again.

Her answer was a moan and to lift her ass up on his downward thrust.

He did it again. And again. And she met him thrust for thrust, moaning and squirming under him as he pounded into her. Her tits bounced with every thrust and Greg couldn't take his eyes off her.

When she brought her hands to her chest and squeezed her tits, he lost it. Greg pushed inside of her deeper than he'd been so far and held himself there as he came. It felt as if he would never stop coming, and even as he fell down on top of her, he felt one more spurt of come coat her insides.

"Fuck," he said as he struggled to keep his weight off of her.

"Yes, sir," she said smugly, "That's what we did."

Forcing himself to move, Greg pulled out, ignoring her sound of dismay, and brought her to the floor. "What are you—Greg!" she exclaimed.

But Greg ignored her. He kneeled between her legs and pushed them apart. Her folds were slightly red from their vigorous lovemaking, but it was his come that was leaking out of her that had him transfixed.

"It's been a long time since I've seen this," he told her, not taking his eyes from her pussy.

"What?"

"It's been years since I've had sex. Karen was too sick to be interested in sex when she was undergoing treatment, not that I was interested either. I was too worried about her." Greg wasn't sure he should be talking about his deceased wife with his new girl-friend, but he couldn't shut up. He caught some of his come and brought it up to her clit, massaging her as he continued to talk. "I'd forgotten how beautiful this is. It's sexy as fuck," he told Sheridan.

Her legs opened wider and as she clenched at his touch, more come leaked out of her. "Greg," she moaned.

"I came too fast," he told her. "But I'll get better after having you a couple hundred times." He heard her chuckle but ignored it. "I promise, though, that I'll always take care of you. You come first—and last. Always."

And with that, he continued to manipulate her clit. A wet spot was forming on her carpet under her ass, but Greg didn't care. He'd steam her carpet tomorrow, and every day for the rest of his life if she gave him this. And it was a gift. A beautiful, sensual, amazing gift.

She lay under him, her arms over her head, giving him all of her, without a moment's hesitation and without seeming to be embarrassed about what he was doing.

Within a minute, Sheridan was shaking under him with her second orgasm of the night. He pressed a finger inside her body as she came, loving how tightly she gripped him and how wet and hot she was. After she'd stopped shaking, he slowly pulled his finger out of her body and caressed her gently. He reached up and grabbed a blanket they'd just christened from the back of the couch and covered her with it.

"Stay here. I'll be right back."

She grunted an okay and kept her eyes closed as he slowly stood. Feeling more emotions than he'd felt in years, Greg stood and headed for her kitchen. Not caring that he was butt-ass naked, he wet a paper towel with warm water and brought it back to where Sheridan lay.

He proceeded to clean her pussy, which made her squirm, then asked, "You ready for bed? It's late."

She nodded and he helped her stand. She led

him to her room and they both climbed into her bed. Without prompting, she put her head on his shoulder and Greg wrapped his arm around her. One of her legs hitched up over his thigh and he sighed in contentment. He'd missed this. The closeness of being with someone else.

"Thank you," Sheridan whispered after several minutes had passed.

"For what?"

"For coming back."

Greg smiled. "You don't have to thank me for that," he told her. "Not when it was a foregone conclusion. You're mine, Sheridan Temple."

He felt her smile against his chest. Her fingers lightly brushed his chest hair as she caressed him.

"Are you mine?" she asked.

"Abso-fucking-lutely," he told her.

"Good."

"Good," he agreed.

"What do you want for breakfast?" she asked sleepily.

"Whatever you want to make," he told her. "As long as you do it naked."

But she didn't hear him. Her light snores telling him she'd already fallen asleep.

* * *

hree days later, while Sheridan was in Greg's bathtub relaxing after a vigorous afternoon of lovemaking, his cell phone rang. He was in the kitchen preparing a snack for them. Sheridan was going to head out to work in an hour or so and he wanted to make sure she had something in her belly before she went. He'd meet her there later and walk her back to his condo.

It hadn't been that long since their amazing first night together, but Greg felt as if he'd known her forever. They liked the same kinds of foods, for the most part they enjoyed the same movies, and they were more than compatible in bed.

Many people would consider him past his prime, but Sheridan made him feel like a new man. A better one. He'd been given a new lease on life and he wouldn't screw it up. Sheridan would marry him, eventually. But for now, they were simply enjoying living.

"Hello?"

"Lambert!" Vice President Warren Angelo drawled. "You ol' dog, you. I heard you've got yourself a new lady friend."

"Word travels fast," Greg complained.

Warren chuckled. "This *is* Washington, you know."

"Right. What's up?"

"Can't I just call to say hello?"

"No. Now, what's up?" Greg repeated. He was friends with the Vice President, but not the kind of friends who would just call each other out of the blue to chat about nothing.

"Got a call from Benedict Hughes at the CIA. He's real happy about the job you did with the Ghost Ops project. He'd like to discuss with you the possibility of—"

"No," Greg interrupted.

"You don't know what I'm gonna say," Warren countered.

"The answer's still no," Greg told him. "I took the Sleeper SEAL assignment because I was at loose ends. I didn't know if I was coming or going and needed something to do."

"We need you, Greg," Warren said quietly.

"All due respect," Greg said. "I served my country, Warren. More than served. I have the commendations and medals...and scars...to prove it. I'm ready to move on. To only worry about my woman and if she's got what she needs to be happy and healthy. I want my biggest worry to be whether or not to have French toast or cereal for breakfast. I want to take a cruise. Relax. Not have to worry where my men are and if they're in trouble or not. I deserve that. As does Sheridan."

Warren was silent for a heartbeat on the other end of the line. Then he sighed. "I get it," he said, resigned.

"Good. I know the fight against terrorism is never going to end. There's always going to be someone out to get us. But I'm done."

"Understood."

"I wish you and Ben the best of luck. There are a lot of good men, former SEALs if that's your preference, who will gladly do whatever's needed to help protect our country. But the only person I have the desire to protect from here on out is Sheridan."

"You're a lucky man."

"I am," Greg immediately agreed. "You gonna get in trouble over this?" The last thing Greg wanted was for the Vice President to get an ass chewing from the President over not getting his assistance.

But Warren chuckled. "Fuck no. Like you said, there are a lot of other men who'll gladly take the money we're willing to pay them to work for us."

"Good."

"She it for you?" Warren asked.

"Yes."

"I expect an invitation to the wedding," the VP said.

"We're eloping," Greg told him, deciding on the spot. If Sheridan agreed to become his wife, there was no way he was going to expose her to the politics that would come with a big Washington, DC, wedding. Hell, the President himself would probably expect to be invited, along with at least half the senate and the House of Representatives and most of the higher-ups in the CIA. No way in fuck was he going to put that big of a bullseye on Sheridan. If she wanted a white dress and the entire wedding, she'd get it, but it'd be as far away from the bullshit politics of DC as he could get them.

Warren chuckled again. "Smart man. But seriously, you need anything, all you gotta do is ask."

Greg nodded. He'd been told the same thing by each and every one of the Sleeper SEALs he'd recruited over the last year to fight and eradicate terrorism. Theirs was a tight-knit group, but he was just as happy keeping that life separate from the one he was building with Sheridan.

"Thanks." Greg heard Sheridan walking around in his bedroom and told Warren, "I gotta go."

"Have a wonderful life," the VP told him. "Seriously."

"I plan on it," Greg said, then clicked off the phone and threw it on the counter. Looking at his watch, he saw that Sheridan still had forty-five minutes before she had to go to work. That was plenty of time.

She loved the way his beard felt against her inner thighs as he ate her out...and he had a hankering for another taste of his woman.

He walked toward his bedroom, unbuttoning his shirt as he went. Putting all thoughts of Sleeper SEALs, the CIA, and terrorists out of his mind. The only thing he was concerned about was getting his woman naked and under him.

He was getting a second chance to have someone to love for the rest of his days and he didn't want to waste one second of it.

ALL of the author who have written in the Sleeper SEAL series want to say THANK YOU for reading our words. This was a fun project for all of us, but it wouldn't have been possible without YOU!

*

Make sure to pick up ALL the books in the Sleeper SEAL series. These can be read in any order and each stands alone.

Protecting Dakota by Susan Stoker

Slow Ride by Becky McGraw

Michael's Mercy by Dale Mayer

Saving Zola by Becca Jameson

Bachelor SEAL by Sharon Hamilton

Montana Rescue by Elle James

Thin Ice by Maryann Jordan

Grinch Reaper by Donna Michaels

All In by Lori Ryan

Broken SEAL by Geri Foster

Freedom Code by Elaine Levine

Flat Line by J.M. Madden

eep reading for the first few chapters of *Protecting Dakota by Susan Stoker*, the first book in the Sleeper SEAL series, and the last book in the SEAL of Protection Series.

Also by Susan Stoker

SEAL of Protection Series

Protecting Caroline

Protecting Alabama

Protecting Fiona

Marrying Caroline (novella)

Protecting Summer

Protecting Cheyenne

Protecting Jessyka

Protecting Julie (novella)

Protecting Melody

Protecting the Future

Protecting Alabama's Kids (novella)

Protecting Kiera (novella)

Protecting Dakota

Delta Force Heroes Series

Rescuing Rayne

Assisting Aimee - Loosely related to DF

Rescuing Emily

Rescuing Harley

Marrying Emily

Rescuing Kassie

Rescuing Bryn

Rescuing Casey

Rescuing Sadie (April 2018)

Rescuing Wendy (May 2018)

Rescuing Mary (Oct 2018)

Badge of Honor: Texas Heroes Series

Justice for Mackenzie

Justice for Mickie

Justice for Corrie

Justice for Laine (novella)

Shelter for Elizabeth

Justice for Boone

Shelter for Adeline

Shelter for Sophie

Justice for Erin

Justice for Milena

Shelter for Blythe (June 2018)

Justice for Hope (Sept 2018)

Shelter for Quinn (TBA)

Shelter for Koren (TBA)

Shelter for Penelope (TBA)

Ace Security Series

Claiming Grace

Claiming Alexis

Claiming Bailey

Claiming Felicity

Mountain Mercenaries Series
Defending Allye (Aug 2018)
Defending Chloe (Dec 2018)
more to come!

Stand Alone
The Guardian Mist
Nature's Rift
A Princess for Cale
A Moment in Time- A Collection of Short Stories
Lambert's Lady

Special Operations Fan Fiction
http://www.stokeraces.com/kindle-worlds.html

Beyond Reality Series
Outback Hearts
Flaming Hearts
Frozen Hearts

Writing as Annie George:
Stepbrother Virgin (erotic novella)

ABOUT THE AUTHOR

New York Times, *USA Today* and *Wall Street Journal* Bestselling Author Susan Stoker has a heart as big as the state of Texas where she lives, but this all American girl has also spent the last fourteen years living in Missouri, California, Colorado, and Indiana. She's married to a retired Army man who now gets to follow *her* around the country.

She debuted her first series in 2014 and quickly followed that up with the SEAL of Protection Series, which solidified her love of writing and creating stories readers can get lost in.

If you enjoyed this book, or any book, please consider leaving a review. It's appreciated by authors more than you'll know.

www.stokeraces.com
susan@stokeraces.com

PROTECTING DAKOTA
SAMPLE

BLURB

Dakota James' life has become the stuff of nightmares. The leader of the Ansar al-Shari'a terrorist group has become obsessed with her, determined to take her as his wife. On the run, she'll have to pin her hopes on the retired SEAL charged with finding and stopping Aziz Fourati before he can carry out plans to bomb more US airports.

Recently recruited to join a sleeper SEAL team

tasked with fighting terrorism on US soil, Slade "Cutter" Cutsinger, with the help of some Special Forces friends, has located the one woman who can identify the deadly Ansar al-Shari'a leader. That was the easy part. Keeping her safe proves more difficult than anyone ever imagined.

When she and her new friend, Caroline, are kidnapped by the terrorist group, Dakota can only pray Cutter and the SEALs will reach them before they're taken out of the country—and away from Cutter forever.

** *Protecting Dakota* is the 9th book in the SEAL of Protection series. It is also a part of the "Sleeper SEAL" connected series. Each book is a stand-alone, with no cliffhanger endings.

CHAPTER ONE

"HEY, WOLF, HOW'D IT GO?" Slade "Cutter" Cutsinger asked the SEAL as he entered the office on the Naval base.

"I'd tell ya, Cutter, but then I'd have to kill you," Wolf joked as he smiled at Slade.

It was a long-running joke between the two men. Slade was a retired SEAL himself, now working as a contractor for the Navy. He worked directly under Patrick Hurt, Wolf's commander. Slade probably knew more about the mission Wolf and his team had been on than Wolf did himself.

"The commander's waiting in his office for a debrief," Slade told the other man with a chin lift, indicating the door to his right. "All good at home? Caroline okay?"

"She's good," Wolf told him. "Thanks for asking.

And I should've said something before now, but I appreciate you checking on her during that last mission. She's used to them, as much as she *can* be used to her spouse leaving for who-knows-where for who-knows-how-long. She told me you helped make her and the others feel better about that mission. You know if you ever need anything, all you've got to do is ask."

"I do know, and it's appreciated," Slade told him.

He hadn't ever worked in the field with Wolf or the other guys on his team, but he respected the hell out of all of them. They were extremely successful on their missions, didn't take absurd chances, and most importantly to Slade, all took care of their families. And by "take care," Slade meant they realized how precious their women and children were and worked their asses off to make sure they knew it. They didn't sleep around on them. If they were running late on a mission, Wolf always made sure Slade checked up on their families. And they had tracking devices on their women, just in case.

Slade wasn't supposed to know about the trackers, but his friend, Tex, had let that little gem slip one night when they were shooting the shit on the phone. Slade had worked on a team with Tex before he'd been medically retired, and hadn't ever found another man for whom he had more respect. When he'd found out about Tex marrying, and then adopting a child from Iraq, he'd been almost as proud for the man as Tex probably was himself.

They'd been talking on the phone one night and Tex had told him that his wife, Melody, had given birth to a little girl named Hope, then he'd told Slade that he'd be damned if any of their enemies got their hands on his baby. With his wife's approval and encouragement, he'd had a bracelet made for his daughter to wear with a tiny tracking device. That's when he'd let the cat out of the bag about the women who belonged to Wolf's team also voluntarily wearing similar jewelry.

Slade had felt a little melancholy that he hadn't ever found a woman he cared about enough to want to protect like that...and who would let him. His ex, Cynthia—not Cindy; God forbid someone call her Cindy—didn't have much interest in anything he did and by the end of their four-year marriage, the feeling was definitely mutual.

All his life, he'd wanted to feel a special connection with a woman. For some reason, he had a feeling he'd just know when he met her. In his twenties, he hadn't been too anxious to find her because he'd been young and eager to make a difference in the Navy. In his thirties, he was ready to settle down, even though he was neck deep working on the SEAL teams. And now, in his late forties, he felt way too old to try to start a serious relationship. He figured he'd lost his chance.

So now he was a confirmed bachelor who kept tabs on the families of the SEALs that worked for Commander Hurt instead.

Mentally shrugging, Slade tried to concentrate on the paperwork in front of him. He missed the action of being on a SEAL team, but he was definitely too old to do the work of the younger men anymore. He gladly left it to them.

The phone next to him rang, and Slade answered. "Cutsinger. How may I help you?"

"I'm looking for Slade Cutsinger. Is this he?"

Slade didn't recognize the voice, but he definitely recognized the authority behind the words.

"Yes, Sir. I'm Cutsinger."

"This is retired Navy Commander Greg Lambert. Is this line secure?"

Slade was taken aback. He didn't remember ever working with a Greg Lambert, and he had a good memory. "No, Sir, it is not. If you need to talk to Commander Hurt, I recommend—"

"It's you I need," Greg interrupted. "I'm going to

give you a phone number. I expect you to call me tonight from a secure line. I have a proposition for you."

"No disrespect, Sir, but I don't know you," Slade said, having trouble keeping his tone professional. He didn't mind taking orders, but usually he knew the person who was giving those orders.

"You don't, but we have a mutual friend who speaks highly of you."

When he didn't continue, Slade asked, "A mutual friend?"

"John Keegan."

Fuckin' A. Tex. What the hell had the man gotten him into now? "He's one of the best men I've ever met," Slade told Greg honestly.

"Ditto. Got a pen?"

"Yeah." Slade dutifully jotted down the number he was given.

"Needless to say, this is a highly sensitive matter. John assured me that you were discreet and would be extremely interested."

"At least he's half right," Slade mumbled, and ignored the chuckle on the other end of the line. "I'll call around nineteen hundred, if that's all right."

"I'll be waiting." And the former commander ended the call without another word.

Slade slowly hung up the phone on his end, lost in thought. He tried to quash the spark of interest that flared deep in his belly, but didn't quite succeed. Working as a contractor for the US Navy kept his toe dipped into the dangerous waters he used to swim in, but it wasn't the same. Somehow, he knew that whatever Lambert had to say to him tonight would change his life. Whether or not it was for the better remained to be seen.

"What the fuck have you gotten me into now, Tex?" Slade asked as soon as his friend picked up the phone.

"Hello to you too, Cutter. How's the weather out there in California? Let me guess, you're sitting on the balcony of your apartment watching the ocean and wishing you weren't bored off your ass."

"Asshole," Slade said with a smile. Tex knew him too well. That's what happened when you worked side by side, getting shot at and saving each other's lives too many times to count. "I got a call from a former Commander Lambert today. He said you two talked about me."

"Not beating around the bush, I see," Tex said.

"I'm supposed to call him back in thirty on a secure line," Slade told his old teammate.

"Gotcha. Lambert is one of the good guys. Worked with him a few times. He has a new job, under the table, and wanted the names of some of the best of the best former SEALs I knew. You were at the top of that list."

"Under the table?" Slade asked. "Not sure I like the sound of that."

"Nothing we haven't been involved with before," Tex reassured him. "Hear him out."

"You been briefed on this job?"

"No. I know Lambert wanted to ask me to help out, but with Hope being so young and Akilah still settling in, I didn't want to do anything that would take me away from home," Tex told him.

Slade got that. If he had a wife and new baby, not to mention a recently adopted teenager, he wouldn't want to leave home either. Feeling restless, he got up and went into his apartment. "You have your hands full with all the teams you work with as well," Slade told his old friend.

"That I do. But I love it. I enjoy being involved in all aspects of our Armed Forces. But it's more than that. I do it to keep the men safe so they can get home to their families."

"It's more appreciated than you'll ever know," Slade told Tex.

As if uncomfortable with the turn in conversation, Tex replied, "That being said, even though I'm not the man for this job, you need anything, you better call. You know no one can find needles in haystacks better than me."

"I don't know, man. I hear there's a chick in Texas who's giving you a run for your money," Slade teased.

"I'll deny it if it comes up later, but that's no lie," Tex said immediately. "Beth is amazing, and she's been able to hack into some places I wouldn't even have tried."

Glancing at his watch, and seeing his time was up, Slade reluctantly said, "Gotta run. Appreciate the head's up and the confirmation that this is on the up and up."

"Anytime. I wasn't kidding, Cutter," Tex said in a hard voice. "You need *anything*, you call. I don't know what Lambert has up his sleeve, but I'm guessing since he didn't brief me when he called, he wants whatever he's asking to be on the down-low... meaning you working alone since you're retired, but nothing is ever fucking solo when it comes to my teams."

"I'll see what he has to say and make the decision whether or not to bring in anyone else," Cutter told Tex. "But I hear you. I'll call if I need you."

"Good. Later."

"Later," Slade echoed and clicked off the phone. He put his personal cell down on the arm of the chair he was sitting in and took a deep breath. Inhaling the scent of salt and sea drifting through the open balcony door, he took a moment to try to calm his mind and body. The pesky feeling that his life was about to change was relentless.

Slade thought about his life. He liked it...for the most part. His oceanside apartment was perfect for him. Not huge, not tiny. He'd saved up his money while he was active duty, and his retirement check wasn't anything to sneeze at. He had a fancy-ass 4K television in the living room behind him, good friends he worked with who he had drinks with every so often, and he could be in the ocean swimming in three minutes, if he was so inclined.

His family was good. His sister, Sabrina, was married with three kids, and his brother also had a wife and two kids. His siblings were both younger than he was, and lived on the other side of the country. He didn't see his nieces and nephews often, but when he did, it was as if no time at all had passed.

He missed his parents, but he'd never had the kind of relationship with them where they'd communicated on a regular basis.

But Slade had to be honest with himself. He was lonely. He had a great apartment, a good job, but no one to share his life with. He'd tried online dating, *that* had been a disaster, and he was way too fucking old to pick up chicks at *Aces Bar and Grill,* the notorious hangout for current and former Navy SEALs. It had become less of a pick-up joint since it was now owned by Jessyka Sawyer, the wife of one of Wolf's teammates, but a bar would always be a bar and there would always be women trolling for a one-night stand or the chance to snag a military guy, and men hoping for a quick hook-up.

Without giving himself a chance to get any more morose than he already was, Slade picked up the secure cell phone he'd been issued by the Navy so he could talk to Commander Hurt and the SEALs under his command, and brought it back out to the balcony with him. He dialed the former Commander Lambert's number.

"Right on time," the commander said as a greeting. "Bodes well for our working relationship."

"I'm not sure I *want* a working relationship with you," Slade told him honestly.

"This line is secure, correct?" Greg asked.

Irritated that he'd think for a second he'd call on one that wasn't when the man had made it more than clear he wouldn't talk otherwise, Slade bit out, "Yes."

Greg chuckled. "Had to ask. No offense intended. You talk to John?"

"Just hung up with him," Slade confirmed.

"Figured. I'm just going to get right down to it, if you don't mind."

"I prefer it, actually," Slade said, his body tensing with whatever he was about to hear.

"I'm in charge of a new initiative, a secret one, to take down sleeper cells of terrorists around the country. The fuckers are getting the drop on us, and it needs to stop. I've been authorized to mobilize my own brand of sleeper cells...retired SEALs."

Slade wasn't sure he understood. "And?"

"And I want *you*, Cutter. I've read your file. I know your strengths and weaknesses. I've spoken with John and some of your other teammates. You're levelheaded and you gather all the intel before jumping into anything. You're determined and have a love for your country that isn't matched by many people. But more importantly, you've been successful on your own."

"I was *never* on my own," Slade protested. "Not once. Even if I went in to get a hostage, my team was at my back."

"I know that." Greg backed off a bit. "What I meant was that when the shit hit the fan, you didn't panic. You simply changed to Plan B...or C, D, or E. I need you."

Slade took a deep breath and let it out slowly. He was curious. Dammit. "Tell me more," he demanded grumpily.

"Six months ago, there was a bombing at LAX."

When the other man didn't elaborate, Slade prompted, "Yeah? I remember it. There was one bomber, he took a handful of hostages. The building was in the process of being evacuated, but the fucker blew himself up, along with all of the hostages, before everyone was out. Ansar al-Shari'a took responsibility."

"Correct. That's what was reported in the news," Greg said.

The hair on the back of Slade's neck stood on end. "That's what was reported on the news?" he repeated.

"Yes. Internet chatter has been extremely active. The bomber was a college kid. He'd been recruited online. The leader's name is Aziz Fourati. Government believes he's Tunisian, and based on the success of the LAX bombing, he's actively recruiting more soldiers. He wants to duplicate his success...on a national level."

"Jesus," Slade swore. "If we thought 9/11 was bad, if he's successful, he could cripple transportation in this country for months."

"Exactly. But that's not all."

"Fuck. What else?"

"He was there," Greg said flatly.

"Where?"

"At the bombing. He was one of the so-called hostages. Gave a speech and everything right before the kid pulled the trigger and blew everyone sky-high."

"How do you know?" Slade demanded.

"All security cameras at the airport were jammed right before everything went down. So there's no public video of anything that happened inside, but someone's been posting audio and video on the Dark Web of his speech on the Internet, and using it as a recruitment tool."

Slade knew there was more. "And? Jesus, spit it out."

"Besides Fourati, who slipped out right before the bomber let loose, there was one other survivor."

The words seemed to echo across the phone line. "What? *Who*?"

"Her name is Dakota James. She was supposed to be flying to a conference in Orlando that day."

"There wasn't ever anything in the newspaper," Slade protested. "How do you know for sure?"

"I've got copies of the propaganda videos Fourati has been sending to his minions. She's there, but her body wasn't one of those found when the pieces of that section of the airport were sorted. Lo and behold, she showed up at work the next week with a broken arm. Told her co-workers she'd fallen down a flight of stairs."

"So, what's the deal? What'd she say about the bombing?"

"That's just it," Greg told Slade. "She's in the wind."

"She's gone? What about her job?"

"Quit."

"Just like that?" Slade asked.

"Just like that," Greg confirmed.

"You think she's involved? That what you need me for?"

"No. We don't think she's involved, but we have nothing on Fourati. We have no photos, no videos that show his face. Nada. Zip. Zilch."

"But Dakota James saw him," Slade concluded.

"Exactly. We need her. Fourati has to be stopped before he can carry through with his plan. As far as we can tell, right now he only has a handful of men he's recruited, but the more he gets, the more his plan can snowball."

"You want me to find her."

"Yes. Find her. Get a description of Fourati, then track that asshole down and eliminate the threat."

Ah, there it was.

Slade had been waiting for confirmation that the former commander wanted him to kill for his country once again. The thought should've been repugnant. He'd left that part of his life behind. But then Slade remembered the pictures of the ruined section of the airport. Remembered the pictures and videos of the victims. A mother traveling with her three-month-old baby. The couple celebrating their fiftieth wedding anniversary by flying to Hawaii for a two-week vacation. The business men and women who were caught in the crosshairs of a terrorist.

The resolve to take down the asshole responsible solidified in his belly.

He opened his mouth to agree to take the job, when Greg spoke again. "There's one more thing..."

Ah, shit.

"Fourati has decided that Dakota James is his." Lambert's voice was matter-of-fact.

"What? How does he even know her?"

"Apparently, he saw her in the crowd at the airport, and whatever happened between them made him decide that he wants her for his own. This is why we think she ran."

"Fuckin' A," Slade swore. "She obviously didn't want to be a terrorist's plaything."

"Apparently not. From what we've been able to intercept and decode, he's on her trail."

"Where is she?" Slade demanded. The thought of the poor woman surviving a terrorist bombing, only to be on the run because said terrorist wanted her for his own, was too much for his psyche. His team had told him on more than one occasion that he had a knight-in-shining-armor complex, but Slade didn't care. He loved women. All kinds. Short, tall, fat, skinny, it didn't matter. When push came to shove on a mission, if it involved a woman, Slade was made point. He did whatever it took to protect the women and children.

"That's the thing. We don't know."

"What *do* you know?" he bit out impatiently. "From where I'm sitting, it's precious little. You know there was a woman, and her name, and that she quit her job, but that's about it."

Greg didn't even sound the least bit upset. "That's why we need you. Find Dakota. Get her to tell you what Fourati said before his soldier blew himself up. Figure out what that fucker looks like so we can find him, shut down his dot-com operation, and get one more terrorist off our streets. Yeah?"

"What backup do I have?" Slade asked, knowing he was going to say yes, but wanting as many details as he could get before he did.

"None," was Greg's answer. "Well, none officially. You can call me and I can get you information. But as far as the operation goes, you're on your own. This is an unsanctioned op. If you get caught, you're also on your own. The US government will not bail you out and, if asked, will deny any responsibility for anything."

Slade wasn't surprised in the least. He'd expected that. "Compensation?"

Greg named a figure that made Slade's eyebrows draw up in surprise. Apparently, the government wasn't fucking around.

"I'm in," Slade told him. He wasn't concerned about failing. He'd find Ms. James, get a description of Fourati, kill him, and continue on with his life. He was actually looking forward to the assignment. Not to kill someone, that wasn't something he ever enjoyed, but getting out into the field once more. Using his skills to eliminate a threat.

Once a SEAL, always a SEAL, apparently.

"Good. I've already arranged with Commander Hurt for you to take some time off. Starting tomorrow. There's a relatively new but vetted employee who will be transferred over to your job immediately. Even though he doesn't have your level of clearance, he can still help Hurt keep his head above water until you return. Your replacement has been briefed and your job is secure until you get back."

"Wow," Slade exclaimed. "I shouldn't be surprised, yet I still am. How'd you know I'd say yes?"

"John said you would. I trust him."

Slade mentally nodded. Yeah, he trusted Tex, too.

"Tomorrow at o-eight hundred, a folder will be delivered to your apartment with all the information I have on the terrorist group, Fourati, and, of course, Ms. James. Find her, get the intel, then stop Aziz Fourati once and for all."

"Is there a time limit?" Slade asked.

"Not per se. But time is always of the essence. As

of right now, Fourati doesn't seem to have enough followers to be a viable threat. However, the more recruits he gets, the higher the possibility that someone will be able to take his place and carry out the threat if he's killed."

Slade understood that. So while Greg said there was no time limit, there was.

"Oh, and not only that, Fourati has said that he wants his new wife by his side before the new year hits."

"Fuck," Slade swore quietly. It was almost the end of November. That meant Fourati was getting impatient, and could have a lead on where Dakota was hiding. The urgency of the case just got ramped up. "I'll look for that folder," Slade informed him.

"Thank you, Cutter," Greg said, using Slade's SEAL nickname once again, proving he really did know a lot about him. "Your country will never know about this, but they're in your debt nevertheless."

"Is this the number I should contact you at if I have questions?" Slade asked. He knew the deal. He knew no one would ever know how many times he'd killed for the sake of national security. He'd long ago gotten over that.

"Yes. I'll be waiting for updates." And with that, Greg hung up.

Slade clicked off the phone and put his head back on the seat. A million things were racing through his brain. Details about the weapons he'd need, how best to take down Fourati without causing a panic, and how in the world he'd pull it all off on his own.

But the one thing that wouldn't let go, that he kept coming back to, was Dakota James. Where was she?

CHAPTER TWO

"HELLO, Mr. James. My name is Slade Cutsinger. May I speak with you for a moment?"

Slade waited patiently a respectable distance away from the door he was standing in front of. He'd received the information folder the morning after his phone call with the former commander and had read every word, twice.

It wasn't a lot of information to go off of—it was no wonder Greg had called him—but the picture of Dakota James had made his teeth clench and his hands curl into fists.

He'd never had as visceral a reaction to seeing someone before in his life as he'd had when he'd gazed into her green eyes. They seemed to grab him around the throat from the paper. She wasn't classically beautiful, her facial symmetry was a bit off for that, but it was the happiness and glee he saw in her eyes that made him want to know everything about her.

The picture was from the latest yearbook from Sunset Heights Elementary School where she was the principal...or *had been*. She was wearing a dark blue suit jacket with a white blouse underneath. She had earrings in the shape of apples in her ears, and her dark blonde hair was in a bun at her neck. Her makeup was minimal, but still, her eyes were her best feature and needed no enhancement.

Slade had stared at her picture for a full ten minutes, shock holding him immobile as he memorized her facial features. He wanted to see more of her. Wanted to see her body, see how tall she was when she was standing next to him, talk to her—was her voice low or high?—touch her. He'd had a sudden and unmistakable reaction to her photo. What would it be like to actually be in her presence?

Thinking about what Dakota had been through made him growl low in his throat, which shocked him back into awareness of where he was and what he was doing.

He wanted her. It wasn't rational, it wasn't normal by any stretch of the imagination, but there it was. Slade wanted to see her smile at him. Wanted to see her eyes twinkle with joy as she looked at him. Wanted to see her eating across a table from him, and most definitely wanted to see her green eyes open and look sleepily at him from the other side of his bed.

Slade had looked at hundreds of dossiers, seen hundreds of targets, and not once had any ever affected him like Dakota James. He would make her safe if it was the last thing he did.

Intel about Dakota's father had been included in the file he'd received from Lambert. He was in his upper seventies and living in a house just north of San Diego. Not sure if the man would give him any information about his daughter—he actually hoped he wouldn't, that he was being extremely cautious about Dakota's whereabouts—Slade had packed his saddlebags on his Harley just in case, and headed out.

Feeling as if time truly was running out for Dakota and she was in extreme danger, his only goal was to get to her as soon as he could. He couldn't explain the feeling, and if he tried, knew he'd sound insane, but Slade's intuition had served him well for his career on the teams. He wasn't going to ignore it now.

"What are you selling?" Dakota's dad barked

from behind the screen. "I don't need no cookies, I'm fat enough, the election's over, and I don't need my lawn mowed."

"I'm a friend of Dakota's," Slade said.

"Bullshit," he responded immediately. "Dakota wouldn't have a friend like you. No way."

Offended, but also somewhat amused, Slade asked, "Why not?"

"You're too good lookin'," her dad said. "Her friends all wear fucking sweaters and khaki pants. And no way in hell they'd be ridin' a Harley like you've got parked in my driveway."

"My leather jacket gave it away, huh?" Slade asked, trying to keep a straight face. He respected this man. He said it like it was.

"Just a bit. Want to try again and tell me why you're here, askin' about my Dakota?"

"Your daughter's in danger and I'm probably the only person who can get her out of it."

The older man was silent for a long moment, but Slade stood still and let him look his fill. Finally, after what seemed like hours, but was in reality only a minute or so, Mr. James flipped up the little hook holding the screen door shut and said, "It's cold out there. Don't know what you're thinkin', ridin' around on a motorcycle. Come on in."

Letting out a relieved sigh, Slade followed the gray-haired man into the house and stood back as he closed and locked the front door. He shuffled slowly into a small living room toward a beat-up chocolate-brown recliner that had seen better days. The television was on and a show about female killers was playing. Dakota's father lowered the volume, but didn't turn it off, and gestured to the sofa nearby. "Go on. Sit. Don't got any refreshments to offer. I don't snack much and the Meals on Wheels lady hasn't come by yet. Thought you were her, honestly. You want to know where my Dakota is, don't ya?"

"Why do you say that?"

"Because I'm old, not stupid," was his response. "Look, you're not the first person to come knocking on my door asking if I know where my daughter is. I'll tell you the same thing I told them, I don't know where she is. And I wouldn't tell you even if I did."

"Who else has been here asking about her?" Slade questioned, his brows drawn down in concern.

The older man waved his hand in the air. "Government types, police types, people from work...you know, the usual."

Slade wasn't sure about that, but he let it go for now. "Mr. James, I—"

"Finnegan."

"I'm sorry, what?"

"My name's Finnegan. Finn."

"Right. Finn, I think you know that Dakota's in danger."

Slade sat still even though Finn narrowed his eyes and stared at him for a long moment before saying, "Why would I know that?"

Taking a chance that Dakota was close with her father, Slade laid it out for him...well, as much as he could. "You and I both know she's the only survivor of that bombing at LAX. She not only saw things she shouldn't have, she probably heard them too. If I was a terrorist who wanted to make sure my future plans went off without a hitch, I'd want to ensure all ends were tied up in a nice fancy bow."

The silence in the room was deafening.

Finally, Finn asked quietly, "Who did you say you were again?"

"My name is Slade Cutsinger. I'm a retired Navy SEAL. I know Dakota has to be scared. I don't blame her. And Finn, she has reason to be. I'm not bullshitting you about that. I can't tell you much, but I *can* say that Dakota has *nothing* to be worried about with me. My only goal is to help her put this behind her so she can move on with her life. Safely."

"You got ID?"

His lips twitched. Hell if he didn't like this old man. Slade slowly reached for his wallet. He slid out his driver's license and government ID, then leaned over to hand them to Finn.

After several moments of scrutiny, Finn returned them and reclined back into his chair. "See that box on the floor next to the television?"

Slade turned his head and nodded when he saw the beat-up old shoebox sitting under a stack of at least a week's worth of newspapers.

"Get it for me."

Doing as he was told, Slade retrieved it and handed it to Finn.

The old man fingered the top of the box lovingly as he said, "Dakota is all I have. My wife died ten years ago, and me and my girl have taken care of each other. She pays for someone to look in on me every day. Pays for the Meals on Wheels people to bring me lunch and dinner. She even makes sure my bills and mortgage are paid. She's a good girl, and doesn't deserve any of this. All she did was go about her daily business and get thrust into a situation neither of us understand."

"I know," Slade said softly.

"She's not here," Finn continued. "Not in San Diego or LA, and probably not even California. She was real shook up after that airport thing. Didn't say much about it, but told me enough that I put two and two together. Then something happened at her school, though she wouldn't tell me what. A couple of days later, her apartment complex burned to the ground. Newspapers said it was some idiot burning candles in an apartment, but I'm not sure what to believe."

"When was this?" Slade asked.

"September. She was so excited for the new school year, but said she had to quit. That someone was following her and she didn't want to endanger the kids at the school."

"You haven't heard from her at all?" Slade doubted that. Someone who obviously loved her dad enough to make sure he was taken care of wouldn't just completely cut off communication.

"She sends postcards," Finn told Slade as he ran his wrinkled palm over the box once more. "Not often, but sometimes."

"Can I see them?" Slade asked, wanting to grab the box out of the old man's lap and get to work finding Dakota.

"If you hurt her, I swear to God I'll kill you," Finn threatened.

"I'm not going to hurt her."

Dakota's dad continued as if he hadn't spoken. "I don't care who you are or where you hide. I'll find you and put a bullet through your heart. It doesn't matter if I go to jail for it either. I'm old, I'm gonna die soon anyway, but it'd be worth it to kill you if you dare do anything that will make my baby suffer more than she already has."

"I've spent my life fighting for the underdog. I've gone where I've been sent and seen and done things that no one should ever have to," Slade told Finn, looking him straight in the eyes. "But one look at a picture of your daughter, and I knew I'd do whatever it took to make her safe."

Finn held his gaze for a moment, then looked down. He cleared his throat twice, as if trying to compose himself, then held out the box. "They're not signed, but I know they're from Dakota."

Slade took the shoebox from Finn and sat back on the couch. He eased the top off and picked up the first postcard. It was from Australia and had a kangaroo on the front. He flipped it over and saw Finn's address written in a womanly script. As the man had said, it wasn't signed, but there was one word written. "Peace." The postmark was from Las Vegas.

He picked up another. It was a picture of the

Statue of Liberty, and once again Finn's address was on the back in the same handwriting as the first. This one said "Love." It was appropriately post-marked from New York City.

Slade flipped through the rest; there weren't a lot, about ten or so. Each had a different postmark and only one word written on it.

"Do you think she's really traveling all over the country?" Slade looked down at the cards in his hand. "From New York to Florida to Seattle?"

"No," Finn said without any hesitation. "She's getting others to mail them for her."

"But she could be," Slade insisted.

"Me and my girl would watch TV when she came to visit," Finn said, gesturing to the television set older than Slade. "The ID Channel. Mystery, forensic, and murder shows. We used to talk about how people could get away with killing for years before they were caught, without even really trying. Not long after the airport thing, she was here and we were watching one of them murder shows. I could tell something was wrong, but didn't want to pry. She flat-out told me she might have to to lie low for a while. I told her she could stay with me, but she shook her head and said the last thing she was going to do was put her daddy in danger..."

Slade sat patiently, waiting for the older man to regain his composure.

Finally, he cleared his throat and said, "She told me she didn't know how safe it would be to call, and was leery of writing letters with any information in them that could lead anyone to her."

"Postcards," Slade said softly.

Finn nodded. "Postcards," he confirmed. "I don't know where she is, but she's gotten her hands on them postcards from all over. Then she has others mail them when they get home from wherever they're visiting when they meet her."

"And the messages on them? Do they mean anything?" Slade asked.

"It's not code, if that's what you're asking," Finn said. "It's just Dakota's way of letting me know she's fine. Love. Peace. Contentment. Happy. She's trying to reassure me she's okay. But she's *not* okay," Finn said. "Look at that last one. The one with the Grand Canyon on it."

Slade pulled it out and turned it over.

"Fucking ink ran. She was cryin' when she wrote it. My baby was cryin' and I can't do anything about it," Finn said bitterly.

"This one's postmarked Las Vegas," Slade mused. "There was another one from Vegas as well."

Finn simply shrugged. "Told her a father would instinctively know if his little girl was alive. What an idiot I was." The old man pinned Slade with a hard gaze. "I *don't* know if she's alive, if she's in pain, if whoever she thought was following her has caught up to her and is hurting her. She could be hungry, or cold, and I'm sitting here snug and happy in my house and can't do a damn thing about it."

"But I can," Slade said firmly.

"If she's in danger, don't bring her back here," Finn replied. "Just let her know her old man loves her and is thinkin' about her."

"I will, but I have a feeling she already knows." Slade put the items back in the box and ran his finger over the mark on the last postcard where one of Dakota's tears had fallen and smeared the ink. Simply touching the same piece of paper she had somehow made her all the more real to him. He'd fallen hard for the woman in the photograph, but seeing how much she loved her dad, and was loved in return, really struck home for him.

He returned the lid to the box and stood, placing it back by the television stand and replacing the newspapers on top.

Finn pushed himself up and out of the chair and the two men stood toe to toe. Slade was at least five or six inches taller, but Finn didn't let Slade's size intimidate him. "Remember what I said," he ordered gruffly.

"I'll remember," Slade told him. "But I'll say it again, you and your daughter have nothing to fear from me."

A knock sounded and Slade's head whipped around to stare at the front door.

"Meals on Wheels," Finn reminded him. "She's right on time."

Slade nodded, but kept close to Finn as he opened the door just in case. As he'd said, a woman wearing a company jacket stood on the other side. "Hello, Mr. James, it's good to see you today."

"You too, Eve," Finn said and unlocked the screen, letting the woman inside. "I'll be right in, give me a second to say goodbye to my guest."

"No problem. I'll just get this served up," Eve said as she breezed past them, obviously having been inside the house before.

Finn put his hand on Slade's leather-covered arm. "She means the world to me," he said seriously.

"I don't even know her, and I think she means the world to me too," Slade responded, dryly.

Finn laughed then. A dry, rough chuckle that

sounded like it hurt. "That's my Dakota," he said, smiling.

Slade's lips curled up in response and he nodded at the man. He was about to leave when Finn said softly, "She's not going to trust you. You're going to have to prove that you've talked to me. That *I* trust you."

Finn had all his attention now. Slade's lips pressed together as he waited.

"Dakota loves Starbucks. Their peppermint mocha was always her preferred choice this time of year. And donuts. Glazed with that maple frosting shit on top. She won't eat no other kind. You bring those with you when you find her, and tell her I told you they were her favorites. The rest is up to you."

Knowing the old man was right, and that he did need a way to convince Dakota to at least hear him out before she ran, he nodded in appreciation. "Thanks. I'll remember. Can I ask something?"

"Sure."

"Why did you let me in? Tell me all that about Dakota?"

Finn looked at Slade for a long time before he said, "My daughter told me the bad guys might come here pretendin' to be good guys. She warned me not to trust anyone, no matter what they looked like."

The old man paused. "Several have tried to get me to talk. Reporters pretending to be Dakota's friends, people sayin' they're government employees who just have her best interests at heart. Bah—liars, all of them. But you...you weren't lyin' to me."

Slade's lips twitched. His former team members would get a kick out of Finn's assessment of him, especially considering he was always the best liar of the bunch.

"Man ridin' around on a Harley, leather jacket, bags packed...you can't exactly kidnap a woman on a motorcycle. Besides...your eyes told me what I needed to know."

"My eyes?"

"Yeah. You took one look at my Dakota's picture and that was it for you." Finn nodded. "Love is a weird thing. When it hits you, it hits you. I knew the second I saw my late wife that I wanted to spend the rest of my life with her. Take care of my girl, Slade. I've worried about her since she was born. The one thing I want is to see her protected and taken care of when I'm gone. Oh, I know, she can take care of herself, but as self-sufficient as she is, she needs someone who will make sure she eats when she gets busy, give her a backrub when she's had a hard day, and will be there for her when she needs to talk."

Finn's words struck Slade hard. Yes. That's what he'd wanted all his life. To have a woman by his side and to be the one someone else leaned on.

"Am I wrong?"

"You're not wrong," Slade said "I'm not going to stand here and tell you that your daughter and I will get married and all your worries are over, but I *am* telling you that I'll do everything in my power to make her safe and allow her to return to her normal life. After that?" He shrugged. "It's up to her. But, if my reaction to her picture was any indication, I'm going to do what I can to convince her to let me be a part of her life."

"That's why I let you in. Why I told you what I did," Finn said, then stuck out his hand. "Good luck. Make my baby safe."

After a final handshake, Slade strode toward his Harley in the driveway, knowing Mr. James was watching him as he did so. He swung a leg over the leather seat and grabbed his helmet.

He began to buckle it when Finn said loudly from the doorway, "You got two of those? Because if you plan to have a passenger, I expect her head to be protected."

Slade grinned, despite the seriousness of the situation. Without a word, he twisted his body and unsnapped one of the saddlebags. He pulled out an identical helmet to the one he was wearing, except a size smaller, and held it up for Finn's inspection.

"Good," was all Finn said, before backing into his house and closing the door.

Slade stowed the extra helmet he'd bought specifically with the intention of having Dakota James on the back of his bike and turned to face the front. He backed out of the drive and headed for the highway. He'd call Tex as soon as he could and let him know he was on his way to Vegas, but first he needed to beat the LA traffic out of town. I-15 to the Nevada border was always a crapshoot this time of year. Starting his search in Las Vegas was a given, as there were two postcards with that postmark.

Whether or not Dakota was there wasn't quite as certain, but one thing was clear...Slade was more determined than ever to find her and keep her safe. Any woman who cared enough about her father to try to reassure him she was all right while on the run from terrorists was someone he wanted to know. But because it was *Dakota* who'd done it...she'd just blown away any doubts he'd had about her. He'd find her, make her safe, then hopefully convince her to give an old retired SEAL like him a chance.

CHAPTER THREE

"HAVE you ever seen an alien out here?"

Dakota James forced a smile and turned to face the tourist. She was working the afternoon shift at the Little A'Le'Inn in Rachel, Nevada, and got asked this exact same question at least once a day. But she really couldn't blame them. They *were*, after all, right outside Area 51 in the Nevada desert, and the small diner she worked at had gone out of its way to put every kitschy piece of alien crap on sale that it could find.

"Nope. Just lots of hungry tourists," she told the teenager, then shrugged in apology for the lame answer and hurried to bring a platter with three plates of hamburgers and fries to the group sitting at a small circular table in the middle of the room.

She smiled and left them hungrily tucking into the food she'd brought them.

Working as a waitress and sales clerk wasn't what she'd had in mind for a life plan when she'd gotten her master's degree in higher education, but life had a funny way of making sure you never got too big for your britches.

Wiping her hands on her apron, Dakota rang up a T-shirt with an alien head on it, a bumper sticker and mug with the A'Le'Inn logo, and an inflatable plastic green alien, then collected money from the pair standing at the register.

She'd been working at the small restaurant/bar for quite a while now and knew it was about time for her to move on. She was grateful that Pat and her daughter, Connie, had hired her. They'd obviously seen the desperation in her eyes when she'd shown up all those weeks ago.

Rachel, Nevada, population around fifty-four, wasn't exactly on the beaten path. People didn't accidentally end up there, and Dakota was no exception. She'd hidden out in Las Vegas for a week, but hadn't liked how dirty the city seemed. Not only that, she always felt as if she was being watched...and since there were so many people, she couldn't figure out if she was *really* being watched, or if it was only in her head.

So she'd left, deciding to make her way across the US, away from California and *him*. She'd stopped for gas just east of Vegas and started chatting with a happy-go-lucky group from Indiana. They'd said they were geocachers, and were headed to the ET Highway. Dakota had no idea what they were talking about, but she'd gotten a crash course soon enough.

Apparently geocaching was kind of like treasure hunting with a GPS. The players downloaded coordinates from a website and followed them to the "treasure." It could be a Tupperware container, film canister, or even a large ammo box. Sometimes there were toys inside, and others only enough room for a log book, which the players were required to sign.

The group was on its way to the ET Highway because there were literally thousands of geocaches alongside the ninety-eight-mile road. They'd talked about the black mailbox, Area 51, the town of Rachel, and the Little A'Le'Inn as if anyone who didn't see them once in their life was absolutely missing out.

So off she'd gone. Instead of heading out of Nevada along Interstate 15, she'd turned north on

Route 93 to Highway 375—also known as the ET Highway.

It'd actually been fun. She'd stopped at the black mailbox, which was now painted white. Enjoyed the desert vistas, mooed at some random cows, and waved at clusters of people she now knew were geocachers who'd randomly stopped along the road searching for the elusive little containers.

Rachel certainly wasn't what she'd been expecting. She thought it would be a typical little town, with a gas station, hotel, and fast food restaurants... but it wasn't. It was literally a pit stop in the middle of nowhere. There were no businesses, other than the A'Le'Inn bar and restaurant. No other places to eat and, more importantly, no gas stations.

She'd planned on seeing what the fuss regarding Rachel was all about, then continuing north to Reno and eventually up into Idaho. Since she'd coasted into town on fumes, she was temporarily stuck. But the second she'd seen the tiny town, she'd decided it was actually a good place to lie low for a while.

Pat and Connie, the owners of the Little A'Le'Inn, had agreed to let her work as a waitress in the restaurant/bar and as a maid for the rooms they rented out—mostly to geocachers on their way through—in the trailers behind the bar. The pay wasn't huge, but it was enough to slowly increase her meager cash reserves before she headed off again.

She'd rented a small room from a local resident, but didn't stay there often. The owner was a smoker who didn't get out much. Dakota had slept in her car most nights, preferring that to being cooped up in a trailer home full of cigarette smoke. Pat caught her one morning and, after hearing why she was sleeping in her car, offered to let her stay in one of the motel's trailers when it wasn't booked.

Working at the motel/bar/restaurant also allowed her to see most of the people who came to town. It wasn't foolproof; if *he* walked in and found her, he wouldn't hesitate to hurt anyone who came to her aid. But the little town suited her. She much preferred the genuine caring nature of most of the people of Rachel to the city folks she'd come into contact with in Vegas.

She'd changed her name to Dallas, thinking it was close enough to her own that she might actually remember to answer to it. The work was monotonous, but the people she met kept the job from being absolutely horrible.

She'd also admitted to Connie that she'd run out of gas, and the other woman had volunteered to bring back enough to allow her to get to either

Tonopah or Warm Springs. Dakota had taken her up on the offer, and felt good knowing she wasn't trapped in the small town. She could leave at any time.

Until now, she'd been enjoying working for cash; it kept her from using credit cards and being tracked through them. Though recently, she felt itchy and nervous. As if someone was watching her again. As much as she hated to just up and leave the quirky little town, it was looking like the time was coming when she'd need to do just that.

"Hey, Dallas, order up," George called from the back. He was the line cook who worked from one to seven. Pat or Connie usually had the morning shift, serving breakfast and early lunch, and after seven, tourists who stopped in could choose from pre-packaged snacks and drinks.

Dakota shook herself and smiled at the older man. Rachel, Nevada, might literally be in the middle of nowhere, but the people who lived and worked there were some of the friendliest she'd ever met. It was too bad she'd be leaving soon.

"*H*ey, Tex," Slade said when his old friend picked up the phone.

"'Bout time you called, Cutter," Tex complained. "I figured you were glued to the slot machines or something. Leaving a message telling me where you're going isn't the same as actually talking to me, you know."

"Yeah, well, I was a bit busy," Slade told him. He'd called two days ago when he'd reached Primm, the border town between California and Nevada. Tex hadn't answered, so he'd left a message about what he'd found out and where he was headed. He'd waited until now to call again because he'd wanted to have some concrete information to share, not simply conjecture.

"I did some checking while waiting for you to call back, and there's been a lot of chatter on the Net about picking up a certain package and preparing for a ceremony," Tex told him.

"Fuck," Slade murmured.

"You got any ideas where she might be?" Tex asked.

"I've been all over this city in the last couple of days. I've shown her picture to everyone, and I might have a lead."

"Yeah?"

"Yeah. You ever been out to Area 51?" Slade asked Tex.

"Nope. Is there anything out there other than desert?"

"Not much. But I'm at a gas station just northeast of Vegas and a clerk says she thinks she remembers someone matching Dakota's description asking about the infamous ET Highway a couple months ago. Said she remembered her because she specifically asked if they had any peppermint flavor for her coffee, and picked up a flier about the road on her way out. I could use your help checking traffic cams for any more recent signs of her in the city, in case this lead is bogus. I thought I'd check out Rachel, Nevada, midway point of the ET Highway, and see if she's been there."

"Already on it," Tex told him. "Started my search right after you left your message. So far, I haven't found anything from the last day and a half, but I'll keep on it. If I find she's been in Vegas recently, I'll let you know."

"Appreciate it."

"You be careful," Tex warned. "With the increased chatter, it certainly sounds as if Fourati has intel on where Dakota might be hiding and could be moving in."

"I will."

"Eyes on your six, Cutter," Tex told him. "If anything feels off, get the hell out of dodge. And don't hesitate to live up to that nickname of yours. Hear me? I'll cover your ass if it comes to it."

"Got it." Slade didn't like the fact that Tex was feeling nervous. If he thought Fourati had a lock on where Dakota was, and had sent some of his minions after her, he was probably right. And Tex telling him not to hesitate to slit someone's throat was telling.

It was Tex who had come up with the moniker during one of their first missions together. Slade had cut the throat of a terrorist who'd had no idea his position had been compromised. It wasn't the first person he'd killed that way, and certainly wasn't the last. Tex had congratulated him on the kill and that was that. The story Slade usually told people, however, was that he was called Cutter because of his last name. It was a bit more politically correct than airing his SEAL kills to polite society.

"I'll call when I can," Slade told Tex.

"You do that. Later."

"Later." Slade hung up and sighed in frustration.

The fact that Fourati was one step behind him wasn't comforting, but at least he was *behind* him, and not *ahead* of him.

Slade slipped the phone back into his pocket and headed into the gas station. If he was going out into the desert, he wanted to top off his tank. He got great gas mileage with his Harley, but had no idea what he'd find when he hit Area 51 and wanted to be ready for anything.

An hour later, Slade turned onto the ET Highway and grimaced. He was suddenly very glad he'd let the gas station attendant talk him into the extra four gallons strapped to the seat behind him. The weather was chilly, but he knew he'd actually lucked out. It could be a lot worse, and he hoped the weather would hold out until he made it to Rachel and, if he was lucky, found Dakota.

The chatty gas station attendant had told him all about how Rachel was the only town along the ET Highway, and they didn't have any services there, only a bar, which seemed wrong to Slade, but nobody asked him. This long desert road wasn't the place to be driving drunk, that was for sure. Not only would it be extremely easy to drive right off the road, it was actually active grazing land for hundreds of cows. The attendant took great delight in telling him two gory stories about motorists who'd hit cows that were standing in the road, minding their own business in the middle of the night.

Taking a deep breath, Slade gave the Harley some throttle as he continued down the long stretch of highway. The faster he found Dakota and got her to safety, the better.

*D*akota grimaced when the bell over the door to the bar tinkled. She was tired and ready to get out of there. She'd been playing bartender for a while now. Doug and Alex, two brothers who worked at the Tonopah Test Range, had come in at the tail end of the day and asked for a couple of beers. They'd said they didn't want any food as they'd grabbed sandwiches at home before heading up to the bar. That had been hours ago, and they weren't acting like they wanted to leave anytime soon.

It was Dakota's responsibility to make sure people got what they wanted to drink, paid, and to try to talk them out of driving if they were out-of-towners. She'd shot the shit with the brothers for a while, but she was bored, tired, and wanted nothing more than to head to the open room in one of the trailers for the night. Luckily, there had been a cancelation that day, which meant she got to sleep in a real bed.

The stress of constantly being on the lookout was getting to her. It was definitely time to head out and find a new place to settle for a while. One more populated than Rachel this time. She'd talk to Pat and Connie tomorrow and let them know she would be moving on.

She smiled in the direction of the doorway—and froze when she saw the man who'd just walked in. He was probably a couple years older than she was. His black hair was graying, but instead of making him look old, it only made him sexier. He had a short beard that was well trimmed and brought attention to his full lips. He had on a leather jacket and an old, worn pair of jeans with black boots. His nose looked like it'd been broken at least once and his cheeks were rosy from the cold, dry air.

He was tall, really tall, at least half a foot taller than her own five-eight. He wasn't skinny, but he wasn't fat either. He was...built. Muscular.

She should've been scared. He could easily over-power and hurt her, but somehow, she knew he wouldn't. How she knew that, Dakota had no idea, but for just a moment, the thought that she knew him flashed through her mind.

That was crazy. She'd never seen this man before in her life, she would've remembered if she had. But the spark of recognition was there, nevertheless.

The man lifted his chin at her in greeting, and Dakota's knees wobbled. How in the hell he could make her want him with a mere chin lift she had no idea, but suddenly, having a wild fling with a stranger sounded like the best idea she'd ever had. It had been a long time since she'd had any sexual feelings about anyone, especially in the last couple of months, but all her worries seemed to drain away simply by looking into his dark eyes.

"Welcome to the Little A'Le'Inn," she said automatically. Business was business, and she didn't want to be the reason the bar got a bad review online. "Grill's closed, but we've got snacks and liquid refreshments. Although if you're continuing on your way to Tonopah, I don't recommend drinking anything alcoholic. It'd be dangerous." Dakota smiled as she said the last, wanting to seem friendly instead of preachy. It would be an absolute shame for this man to come to any harm, that was for sure.

The man's eyes seemed to pierce right into her

soul, as if with one look he knew all her secrets. The scariest thing was that it wasn't an altogether unpleasant thought. She'd never had someone she could lean on to help with troubles in her life. She'd been okay with that, modern woman and all, but in that moment, all she could think was that *this* man would keep her safe. He'd never let anyone do her harm.

Dakota turned her back on him, pretending to wipe off the counter to try to regain her equilibrium.

Out of the corner of her eye, she saw the man saunter into the dimly lit building and gaze around. She'd seen many reactions from tourists who'd wandered into the eclectic bar, but this man had absolutely no reaction whatsoever. It was...odd.

"Nice place," he said, and Dakota's toes curled in her sneakers. His voice was low and growly and she felt it all the way to her tummy. She had no idea why she was reacting to this man's obvious maleness, but she was.

"Yeah. The owners have worked hard to make it...unique."

"Slade," the man said, holding his hand out to her in greeting.

"Oh...uh...I'm Dallas," Dakota said shakily,

almost forgetting her fake name, and tentatively put her hand in his own.

She was half afraid he'd crush hers with his brute strength, but he merely smiled and grasped her palm with a firm, but not bruising grip and said, "It's good to meet you."

Dakota gave him a half smile. "You too."

They stood still for a beat, each looking at the other without blinking, before Dakota reluctantly pulled her hand back. He let go without complaint, but she swore she could feel his touch long after they'd dropped their hands. He had calluses, which made her think about what his hands would feel like on her bare skin. Damn, she had to get it together.

"So, what's it gonna be?" Dakota asked.

"Just a Coke, I think," Slade said.

"What kind?"

"What kind of Coke?"

Dakota chuckled and shook her head in self-deprecation. "Sorry. Habit. I call all soda, 'Coke.' I use it generically. I can get you one," she finished quickly, knowing she was beat red with embarrassment.

"So if someone asks for a Coke, you ask what kind, and they say a Pepsi. Or Dr. Pepper, or something else?" Slade asked with a friendly smile. He leaned his forearms on the scratched wooden bar top in front of him.

For a moment, Dakota wished that it was summer and Slade was wearing a short-sleeved T-shirt. She'd pay just about any amount of money to see his biceps and forearms. She'd bet they were muscular as hell. When he tipped his head and raised his eyebrows as she continued to stare at him, she blushed even harder. "Sorry. Yeah, that's how it works. So you really do want a Coke, right?"

"Yes, please. If it's not too much trouble," Slade said with a smile.

"Of course not. It's my job," Dakota told him, glad to have a reason to go into the back room for a moment. There were a few cans under the bar, but she wanted to get him a cold drink from the refrigerator in the back.

She used the few moments alone to give herself a stern talk. *He's just passing through, Dakota. The last thing you need right now is to get involved with a guy, even if it's only for the night. No matter how sexy he is and how badly you want him. Get ahold of yourself.*

Satisfied that she had her head on straight, Dakota went back into the bar area with a smile on her face and held up the can. "Got it!" Instead of drooling over the fine specimen of a man who was sitting at the bar, she got busy grabbing a glass and filling it with ice. She poured the cola into the glass, concentrating so hard on what she was doing, she jumped when Doug pounded on the bar top down by the cash register.

"We're gonna get out of your hair, Dallas."

Dakota looked up and nodded, putting down the half-empty can because her hands were shaking too hard to finish. She glanced around and met Slade's concerned eyes.

"You okay?" he asked quietly.

Dakota nodded quickly and pushed the glass and can of soda over to him. "Here ya go. Excuse me."

He nodded and she took the few steps to the register. She made small talk with Doug and Alex while she rang up their drinks. After they left, the room seemed to shrink. Being alone with Slade made her extremely nervous for some reason. She tucked a stray piece of hair behind her ear and smiled awkwardly at him.

"You worked here long?" he asked.

Dakota shrugged. She'd learned to keep her answers vague. "Not really."

"It's a long way from civilization, isn't it?"

She shrugged again. "It is what it is. I've met

some of the nicest people around. You on your way north or south?"

It was his turn to shrug. "I came up from Crystal Springs, but I'm not sure if I'm going to go back that way or carry on. Anything worth looking at if I go up to Tonopah?"

"Depends on what you like to look at," Dakota told him. "I've heard Goldfield is really interesting, with the history of being haunted and all, but there's not much out here in either direction, if I'm being honest."

"Hmmm. Any place to stay the night around here?" Slade asked.

Dakota swallowed hard. Damn. There went her bed for the night. But she smiled brightly and told him the truth. "You're in luck. There was a cancelation tonight so there's a room available. It's not fancy, you actually share a trailer with another couple, but they checked in about an hour ago and I think they're planning on being up early, so they won't be a bother. The middle is a common space, and the two bedrooms are on either side and have locking doors. It really is private."

Dakota knew she was babbling, but couldn't stop. "It's only forty-five bucks for the night, which is a really great deal. There's hot water and you can use the wi-fi here at the restaurant for free. Breakfast is included. Nothing gourmet, just cinnamon rolls and juice, but again, it's safer to stay than to try to make it all the way up to Tonopah in the dark."

Slade chuckled, and Dakota's womanly parts spasmed at the sound. Jesus, he was beautiful.

"I'll take it. How could I not after that wonderful sales pitch?"

"Sorry. People just tend to turn up their noses because it's a trailer and they have to share it, but I promise it's clean, safe, and totally worth the money."

Slade tipped his head back and chugged the rest of the Coke in the glass. He pulled out a five-dollar bill and slid it over to her. "Sounds good. I'm beat."

"Let me get your change."

Slade waved her off. "Keep it."

"Oh, okay, thanks. If you're ready, I can walk you over to your room."

He looked at his watch. "You're closing?"

Dakota nodded. "Yeah, we're not expecting anyone else tonight and it's dark. The locals know we close up around now."

"Don't want any aliens to wander in when the sun goes down, huh?" Slade joked.

Dakota chuckled even though she'd heard it

before. "Yeah, something like that. If you want, I'll meet you outside in five minutes or so? I need to finish up in here." Actually, she needed to give herself another talking to, but he didn't need to know that.

"Sure. I'll be out by my bike."

Dakota nodded. Her eyes were glued to his ass as he walked out the door. He was definitely a fine specimen of a man. And it figured he'd have a motorcycle, just to amp up the sexiness. She'd never ridden on one, but once upon a time, before she'd gotten old enough to have given up on many of her dreams, she'd imagined what it would be like to sit behind a man, her arms wrapped around him, her chin on his shoulder as the wind blew in her hair and they flew down the highway.

Shaking her head in disgust at herself, she mumbled, "Get ahold of yourself. Jesus, you'd think you weren't on the run from a psycho crazy terrorist or something. You've got no time for mooning over a man. No matter how sexy he is or how much you want to know if his beard is soft or scratchy."

Satisfied with her pep talk, Dakota quickly washed the dirty glasses and locked the ancient cash register. There wasn't a bank in Rachel to take the cash to, and besides, most people paid by credit card anyway.

She hung up her apron and smoothed her hair, securing it back into a bun at the nape of her neck, and walked out the door.

Slade was leaning against his Harley with one ankle resting on the other. His arms were crossed on his chest and he was frowning. Dakota quickly turned and locked the door, making sure the closed sign was clearly visible to anyone who might pull up later. Taking a deep breath, she turned to Slade. "Everything okay?"

He shook his head. "There's no cell service."

"Yeah, sorry. Once upon a time the residents petitioned the big phone companies to put a tower out here, but it wasn't worth the money. And if you ask me, the government put the kibosh on that as well. It's in their best interest to keep things on the down low out here, if you know what I mean. Area 51 and all. If it's any consolation, once you get up to Warm Springs and past the big mountain up there, you'll be in range again. If you really need to get ahold of someone, I could ask Pat—she owns this place with her daughter—if she'll call someone for you. There are a few residents who have satellite phones out here."

Slade shook his head. "No, it's okay. I can wait. I was just hoping to get ahold of my friend and let him know I made it safely and that I'd be spending the night."

"Sorry," Dakota apologized again. "You could probably send him an email later if you wanted. I'll make sure you have the password for the wi-fi. Ready to see where you'll be staying?"

"Don't I need to pay for the room?" he asked.

She waved her hand. "Don't worry about it. You can pay Pat or Connie in the morning. They man the restaurant until I come on in the afternoon."

"Trusting," Slade observed.

Dakota smiled at that. "Yes, they are. Come on, it's around back."

He straightened and turned to grab the handle-bars of his motorcycle. He pushed the bike as they walked silently around the front of the iconic restaurant, past the giant metal spaceship announcing to anyone who passed by that they'd reached the A'Le'Inn, to one of the trailers off to the side of the parking lot.

"Here it is. And I know it doesn't look like much, but I promise it's clean."

"I believe you," Slade told her, holding out his hand for the key Dakota had been playing with.

"Oh yeah, here ya go." She inhaled when her fingertips brushed Slade's palm. He was warm, and she was quickly getting chilly in the desert air. "Right, so there's the entrance, just turn to the right when you enter and that's your room. Sleep well."

"See you later," Slade said as he nodded at her.

"Yeah, okay," Dakota mumbled, knowing he wouldn't. She did her best to avoid the restaurant in the mornings, not wanting to interact with the people who stayed the night, and needing the time to herself. Connie let her use her computer in the mornings, and Dakota used the time to search the Internet for mentions of her name, and to try to see if she could figure out the name of the asshole who was following her. So far, she hadn't had any luck, but it didn't really matter. She knew she was in trouble; the guy had practically told her straight up she would be his. She shuddered at the memory.

Turning and heading for her car, which was behind Pat's trailer, Dakota mentally reminded herself once more to talk to the other woman soon. It was time to go.

---

*T*hree hours later, Slade walked silently past the trailers that were rented out to tourists and headed for where he'd last seen Dakota. She looked exactly like her picture, right down to the bun at the back of her head. At least she'd altered her name a bit; it wasn't much, but it was something. She hadn't tried to disguise herself at all.

But then again, why would she think anyone would follow her to Rachel, Nevada?

The town seemed like it was at the end of the world. Strangers stood out like sore thumbs and she knew exactly who was sleeping where each night. Slade had used the wi-fi to kill time and find out more information on the small town. He knew Dakota wasn't going anywhere, she didn't seem to be suspicious of him at all.

And if he wasn't mistaken, she'd been struck by the same thing he had when she'd lain eyes on him the first time. Slade recognized the look of interest and lust in her eyes, because he knew it was the same look on *his* face when he'd first seen her photo. And as he thought she would be, she was even more beautiful in person. She was curvy, and he estimated her to be around five-eight or nine; her head came to about his chin. Slade knew she'd fit against him perfectly.

She was funny and endearing when she got nervous. He could absolutely see her as an elementary school teacher and principal. It was the uncertainty and uneasiness behind her eyes that really struck him, though. He hated that she was scared, and wanted to hold her tightly and reassure her that he'd make sure Aziz Fourati didn't get anywhere near her. He needed to be smart, but didn't have the luxury of time to let her get comfortable with him. He needed to talk to her about her situation, get her to trust him, and get the hell out of Rachel, Nevada.

The bottom line was that Dakota James was no longer merely a face on a piece of paper. She was a flesh-and-blood woman, and Slade wanted her more than he wanted his next breath. But he wanted to keep her safe more than he wanted, or needed, to have her under him...for now.

He'd been planning to break out the bribe he'd picked up for her in Vegas when they'd been alone at the bar, but she'd seemed too uneasy around him. And he was afraid she'd bolt if he spooked her. So, he was biding his time, and he'd catch up with her in the morning.

Slade really wished he could get ahold of Tex

and find out if he had any information about Fourati, and if he or his cronies were on their way to Rachel, but for now, he was winging it. He didn't trust email to be secure and decided he'd wait.

When enough time had passed, Slade had eased out of the plain and simple room in the trailer and was now looking for Dakota.

The wind blew in from the north and he shivered in the cool night air. Winter was definitely arriving in the valley, and Slade wouldn't be surprised if there was snow in the forecast. Peering around one of the trailers, he grinned. Bingo.

Tex had given him the details on Dakota's car...a two thousand and eight Subaru Impreza. Gray. And it was parked in front of him. She hadn't even taken off her California plates. Slade inwardly grimaced. She didn't have the first clue how to hide. It was both endearing and frightening at the same time. It was a good thing it was *him* there looking for her and not Fourati.

Slade walked silently up to the car and peered in, not expecting to see anything worth his time. He stopped short and stared through the window.

Dakota was wrapped up in a blanket in the driver's seat, only the top of her head and blonde hair showing. She was sleeping in her car.

She was *sleeping* in her fucking *car*.

Slade wanted to hit something. Wanted to bang on the glass and wake her up and read her the riot act. It was cold out there, but honestly that was the least of her worries. What if he'd been Fourati? Or a drunk resident who'd decided she was free game? Yeah, Dakota was tall, but she wouldn't be any match for a drunk, horny guy.

Swearing under his breath at the entire situation and hating himself for not confronting her earlier that evening, Slade turned around and headed back to his room. If he was going to watch over one Miss Dakota James, he needed warmer clothing.

She might not have asked for it, but starting right now, she had a protector. Seeing her sleeping, vulnerable, and probably cold, had ramped up his interest in her from warm to red hot. Dakota needed protecting, and he'd be the man to do so.

And when she no longer needed protecting, he'd still be the man in her life.

T O KEEP READING...CLICK HERE>>>>>

Protecting Dakota

Made in the USA
Middletown, DE
04 August 2021

45407944R00070